Sleigh Ride:

A Winter Anthology

Short stories by:

Megan Barlog

Maria Geraci

Malena Lott

Maggie Marr

Jenny Peterson

Dani Stone

Samantha Wilde

buzz books

ISBN13: 978-0615552330

ISBN10: 0615552331

For more information on the book or to schedule a speaking engagement, discuss a media opportunity or sales, please contact Buzz Books at www.buzzbooksusa.com.

Editor's Note: Buzz Books has made "Sleigh Ride" a Good Read/Good Deed project with a portion of the proceeds benefitting the domestic violence prevention cause through the Alpha Chi Omega Foundation. Thanks for your support.

Table of Contents

Looking like two loving snowballs
in our fuzzy Arctic furs,
Tucked in warm and snug together,
whisking through the winter weather
Where the tinkle of the sleigh-bells
is the only sound that stirs.

—*Katherine Lee Bates, "Goody Santa Claus," 1889*

Monks and Musicians

By Samantha Wilde

Years after the sleigh ride, Jeff and I would debate who came up with the idea. He claimed *I* suggested it, that I'd been browsing through the paper some Saturday morning in January and found an enticing advertisement. I do remember the listing in the paper, how cozy and darling it made it sound: "Snuggle under our thick, soft blankets and ride through the breathtaking woods. Hear an owl. Stop for hot chocolate. Gaze at the stars."

But remembering the ad doesn't make it my idea. I would never have voluntarily gone on a sleigh ride. I don't like the cold and I don't like the snow, and—quite unpopularly, I know—I don't like horses. That infamous sleigh ride certainly didn't improve my feelings for the animal. Besides, a seven-o'clock ride ensured corruption of Bessie's nighttime routine—something I *never* did.

It was Jeff's idea. He showed *me* the ad, which I looked over and said nothing about. Then he showed Bessie the ad. She stared at it curiously before asking: "Where's the pictures?" However smart a girl she may have been at three years old, and she was as clever and articulate as a defense attorney, she could not read.

"A sleigh ride!" Jeff exclaimed, and then he powered up his laptop, found the company on the web and showed Bessie pictures until she jumped up and down with a rallying cry of "Sleigh ride *now!*"

"This is what people do for fun in the winter," he told me later, during Bessie's nap, while we shoveled the walkway from the latest snow, and I protested that I did not want to go out that late, that I was tired, and what if the blankets were dirty or smelly or itchy and woolly? Jeff laughed at me.

The piles beside us were belly button high. The day before, Jeff and Bessie made a couch out of snow long enough for Jeff to lie on while I stayed in, feeling dour and cold, sweeping the floors grudgingly, feeling sorry for myself.

"It will be fun," he promised.

"I grew up in California," I reminded him. "Until last fall, we lived in Atlanta where this much snow would mean a national disaster."

He tossed a snowball playfully in my direction. That's how it was then: I was heavy, he was light. I was somber, he was jovial. I was burdened, he was free.

Not that I think of it so much any longer, except when it snows, which it seems to do all winter, and when Bessie, now a recalcitrant older child who pleads on a regular basis for a horse, asks if we can go on another sleigh ride because the first one, sprinkled with the magic fairy dust of early childhood that colors everything in goodness, was so much fun.

"You slept through most of the ride," I point out to my ten-year-old.

"I remember everything!" she protests, and it always makes me smile, an ironic smile, one Bessie is still too young to read. She remembers nothing, nothing at all, and I remember everything.

I remember the color of the blankets, which, as I feared, were woolly and scratchy and dark. And our driver, Luis, who wore enormous ear muffs and claimed to be hard of hearing long before Jeff and I began arguing—a fortuitous disclosure, as it turned out, so we never had to worry that he was pretending, out of politeness, not to listen to our regrettable conversation.

"We were lucky to get a nearly deaf driver," I said to Jeff that night after we arrived home. He carried Bessie inside, holding her over his shoulder the same way he does the kitchen cloth when he cooks.

"Does it really matter if some stranger knows?" Jeff asked.

"So you hoped for public humiliation?" I said as he slipped inside the door like a snake into our garden rock wall. The outer door slapped into the doorframe with a hollow thud.

As it happened, I ended up liking the actual sleigh ride more than I thought. The woods were peaceful, and at some point, a tiny snow fell on us. Bessie ate a flake off her nose. When she fell asleep in my lap, Jeff leaned over and kissed her still-baby-soft cheek. When he sat up, he sighed— unusual for him, and telling.

"Something happened," I said to him then. He didn't answer. "Jeff?"

We were pulled by two enormous, brown horses—not the pretty, fancy kind, but serviceable horses, well trained, with pitch-black eyes and coarse manes. Their hooves crunched satisfyingly in the snow. It made me think of eating potato chips; it made me hungry. I was always hungry around that time, either hungry or sick, classic signs of morning sickness that I chose to ignore.

I chose to ignore a great deal back then. Like, for example, the way Jeff lie beside me in bed, with such stillness, faking sleep, his eyes fighting to stay closed, his eyelids quivering with the effort. I didn't stop to ask myself why he would pretend to sleep, or why we didn't often have sex, or why he had fun with Bessie as I lingered like an uninvited guest in the doorway while they played. I can blame all that ignorance, with seven years' hindsight, on the sort of oblivion of love and duty that gets visited on all first-time mothers. I could blame it on hormones; I certainly had enough of them hopping around inside of me like one of those amusement park games where the mole pops up over and over while you furiously try to bang it on the head.

"I had sex with Lynn." Bang! He made this announcement as the sleigh gracefully led us into a pine forest, obscuring the half-moon light, so it seemed we had entered a different sort of darkness. In the moment, the symbolism was completely wasted on me. The night could have been a poem! It could have been a blockbuster! It could have been a reality TV show! In fact, I wished it were a reality TV show where reality gets buffered and muted by voyeurism. Nothing's more unrealistic than reality TV. Better yet, if we could have been paid guests on Jerry Springer simply after the money and the thrill of the drama, things would have been so much less *actual.* I would sling a fist in his direction, and he would fall off the sleigh and have a realization while in the midst of a coma, and we would have ten therapy sessions and a happily-ever-after, five-years-later reunion on television where Jerry would ask our daughter if her parents love each other, and she would half-swoon and half-pucker in disgust saying, "They, like, kiss *all* the time."

Hmmpf. This is decidedly *not* what happened. Jeff looked straight ahead as he spoke, making his confession to the horses – to their rear ends, like a horse's ass, I thought to myself then and giggled, which forced him to turn and look at me.

"Lynn?" is all I could manage at the moment, although I would have preferred a string of expletives and a cry like Jane and Tarzan falling off their vine and hitting the hard ground.

"It was only a few times," he said, looking away again. "I love Bessie," he added, which hit like a mortal wound, a worse crime even than the infidelity, this leap to our daughter and with it the omission of the proper statement: "I love *you*, Angie." Never mind the other trite, requisite statements every philandering husband ought to have memorized, the "I'm sorry" or "please forgive me" or "I'll never do it again." We had a child together, a child we adored, and she came first. "I don't want to lose her." Still he talked to the horses' bottoms in a low, whispering voice. The snow stopped falling. He *was* a horse's ass.

"I hate Lynn." Another nonsensical comment, as if it would have made a difference if he'd slept with someone I actually liked – though, let's be clear: Lynn Periwynn leaves a lot to be desired.

"Why do you have to be such a cliché? Sleeping with your secretary!" I scoffed.

Then, at last, what I expected to hear first, "I'm sorry."

"You mean you're sorry you're a cliché, or you're sorry you slept with her?"

"She's not *my* secretary. Technically."

"Right. Well, this is an excellent moment to get technical. I mean, *technically*, she's not all that worth sleeping with, is she? She's got a saggy bottom, for one thing. She's older than both of us, she wears clothes from 1982, she's practically cross-eyed without her glasses on, and she *smokes*. That's so disgusting. What did her breath taste like when you kissed her?"

"Angie--"

"What? You can do it, but I can't talk about it?"

"I made a mistake."

"You *really* made a mistake."

I called my stepmother, Marsha, after we came home, after Jeff slunk into the guest bedroom with his alarm clock in hand. Many years ago, Marsha replaced my mother as a mother on account of the fact that my mother took a permanent vacation to Tibet in order to move on from her divorce. Apparently, she was too wounded to remain in the same country with my father, and told me she needed to seek solace in the hills, with the monks who knew things about pain and recovery. "Perhaps I can find an answer in one of my past lives," she explained. I've never understood what good it would do her given how little attention she paid to her current one. At any rate, I didn't miss her as much as I thought I would have; Marsha had more skills as a mother. She did it better.

"Jeff has always been hopeless. If I swore, which I don't, I would call him a bastard, and he's always been a bastard, you and I both know that." As Marsha spoke, I called up her smell to memory, the faint hint of her rose perfume and stronger scent of some powerful cleaning agent, burned into her skin from years of zealous, impassioned, stainless-steel scrubbing; you could eat out of her kitchen sink. I nearly broke with longing to be near her, except I didn't let myself, not at that moment, not with Jeff in the next room, pious and cold, as though *I'd* done something wrong.

Had Jeff always been a bastard? I thought, as she spoke about my husband of six years, all his failings, all his virtues, the way he dressed in the morning, standing naked in the bedroom, putting on his socks first. He claimed his feet were always cold. I accused him of being a reticent nudist.

"It only happened a few times," I told Marsha.

"Did you say he told you during a sleigh ride?"

"It was a beautiful night."

"That is too much! Completely thoughtless. Did you pay for the sleigh ride? What a waste of money." Marsha never had much extra cash, so I didn't blame her for this pointless complaint. Who cares about money when you can't get the image of your husband and the church secretary out of your head?

"Will I divorce him?" I asked her.

"Angela," she said, a little breathlessly, as though suppressing a chuckle. "Divorce is a sin."

"Yes. I'm aware of that. Tell me again how many husbands you've had?"

She laughed girlishly. "The first three didn't count."

"Besides, I'm not religious." As if religion could make the matter easy to dispose of, easy to endure.

"Yes, darling, but he is."

We hadn't talked about the future during the sleigh ride. We hadn't talked about divorce or how to handle the betrayal. She was the church secretary, and Jeff was the church pastor. How many people had he betrayed with his little one-nighter? How about his whole flock of eighty?

Eventually, during the sleigh ride, I said, "I wish you would get off the sleigh," a line Marsha and I would later laugh hysterically about in that way you laugh when crippled by sorrow – defeated by it, really. "Get off the sleigh and walk home."

"I'll be knee-deep in snow!"

"You're knee-deep in shit as it is."

"You don't have to swear."

"You don't have to sleep with other women. In fact, given your revelation, I think it's time to cut the arrogant, holier-than-thou garbage. Never mind me; you clearly aren't worried what I'll think. What about the *church*? Do you really think they'll want you to preach come Sunday morning, Lynn sitting upright in the pew next to her aging, blind father, like you know something we all don't? Like you're wise?" I laughed, or I cackled. I could feel a scream bubbling up inside of me. Bessie shifted and murmured in her sleep. The horses' feet carried on with their rhythmic crunching, and Jeff placed his head into his hands. "I feel sorry for you."

That first night, he stayed in the house. The next day, armed with the clarity of morning and the brutality of a ten-degree day during which I knew I would be hiding out inside with Bessie all day, I packed Jeff a bag. I told Bessie to wave at him. I wanted her to be awake to see him go. I said he had a conference to attend, as he often did. She smiled. She kissed him.

"Angie," he said as he leaned in toward me, and I walked away.

There wasn't much funny about that first week without him, though Marsha came to stay, and we could not keep from laughing. She made me a cake. She called it a Cheater's Widow Cake.

"I wish I were a widow," I said, digging in to the oozing chocolate center.

"No, you don't." Marsha cut herself a giant piece.

"I don't mean it that way. I don't mean you. Dad would never have cheated."

"That's true. But he did die. Rather thoughtless of him, isn't it?"

"I'm being selfish," I said, thinking of how it must feel to Marsha who lost her husband, my father, four years prior.

"You are being human."

"I might be pregnant," I told her then, and for some reason, that same hysteria came over us. Like two teenage girls confronted with the realities far beyond their comprehension, we snorted through our mouthfuls of cake.

"I'm so happy!" she said, tears streaming down her face, and she hugged me.

"It's awful," I told her, putting down my fork and pushing away the plate. "I don't want Jeff's baby. I hope I'm not. I really, really, hope I'm not."

* * *

At some point, during that sleigh ride, while Jeff and I sat captive in our seats, alternately arguing and lapsing into tense, hard silence, Bessie did wake up. She rolled over onto her back, her head still in my lap, and began to talk about what she saw overhead: the stars, the tree branches, a fairy, a cloud becoming a witch on a broom, a shadow transforming into a large bat with a feathered hat. She registered an owl baby sucking on a pacifier, and a thirsty butterfly catching snow. Jeff didn't stop her fanciful, delightful imaginings. I started pointing out constellations. "There are *real* magic things," I said definitively.

"Why ruin it? You always take away the fun," Jeff said.

Later that night, I would retaliate; I would lean into my sense of insult with gusto. I called him "a failure," a "poor excuse for a man," a "pathetic imitation of a minister," a "lost loser," and a "sorry excuse for a husband." I said other things, too, of course, a wonderful litany, and it felt good to call him every name in the book. I knew I was justified. This wasn't a matter of degree. He had wronged me completely. He had done something unforgivable. I hated him for breaking our vows — and for such a ridiculous woman—Lynn! A woman who occasionally adorns herself with press-on nails!

And Jeff hadn't always been a bastard. The man was a minister. He spent a lot of time thinking about how to do the right thing by other people, holding the hands of dying, old, white heads and leading Bible study for spinsters and half-deaf octogenarians. The sort of people who have too much free time during the day, retired people and unemployed people, and people forgotten by friends. In fact, Jeff made a point to be friends with all the friendless he encountered, despite the fact that they either talked too much, or spit out of the corners of their mouth or never once stopped to ask him a single question about himself.

Jeff made a thing about being selfless, and while I never agreed with his religious beliefs, he loved me anyway. It didn't matter to him. He would sit and read his Bible quietly in the evenings, preparing a sermon, scratching notes into his big, blue pad. He loved his work in the church, leading boring and tedious committee meetings with pizzazz. Returning phone calls in the middle of the night. Making house calls, and standing up every Sunday with his sharply pressed robe, inviting everyone to "the table."

When we first met, I told him, "Jesus isn't for me." And after our first date, I told him: "This won't work. I don't believe in religion."

He laughed. "You don't need to believe in *religion*."

"I don't believe what you believe."

"That's okay," he said, leaning in with a kiss.

Jeff had an ease about him. I didn't need to believe, because he felt assured of his own rightness. We got along despite our differences, though with a slight edge, an underlying assumption that Jeff was right, and I was, if not wrong, somehow not quite there. When my father died, Jeff didn't hesitate. He sat beside me. He held my hand while the grief pummeled me in oceanic waves. It seemed he could weather anything with aplomb. I didn't want religion for myself, but it sure worked well on Jeff. I considered him a better man than most. And don't you have to be? To sit with the lost and the losing and the grieving and the dead, and walk away still able to live passionately?

But *I* didn't like the deep questions and passion terrified me. I didn't bother with it. I let Jeff have it, have all of the big emotions. He talked about meaning and redemption and salvation the way I discussed chicken thighs and junk mail and holiday plans. After Bessie was born, he went on discussing the "holy-moley stuff," as I called it – the divine goulash, the Big Issues – while I debated diaper brands and play-date scheduling and night feedings.

Not that I didn't understand why Marsha considered him equal to the bastard label. His helpfulness often came across as superiority, his eagerness to share his thoughts as pride. Jeff *did* think he had the answers. He had to. He had to stand up every week with them, hold up those answers like a bulletproof vest and say, "No doubt can make it through."

"I'm sick at my stomach," I said, toward the end of the sleigh ride, that interminable sleigh ride, so quaint, thick with romance and loveliness and me imagining Lynn in the throes of ecstasy with her legs wrapped around my husband's pelvis. "I think I'm going to throw up."

Jeff took his head out of his hands. "Really? You better move Bessie." As though I might ralph directly onto my daughter's head!

"If I do it, I'm aiming it your way." He grimaced. A wave hit me and I leaned over the rail and puked into the glistening, glossy white snow.

"Did you really just throw up?" he asked, as I coughed and sat up.

"Are you, the man who just admitted to committing adultery with his church secretary, a man of the cloth, a man who's taken vows before God to honor his wife *and* his congregation, accusing me of lying about *vomit*?"

"Almost there now!" deaf Luis shouted to us from his post at the front of the sleigh.

"Why sick, Mama?" Bessie asked. Later, I would think how preferable her comment was to one she might have made: "What's 'adultery,' Mommy?"

"You got some on her," Jeff accused.

"I did not." I hated him, for that worry, for his pettiness, for his shallow disapproval and disregard. How could he *act* like that when he'd just confessed to adultery?

I leaned close to him, put my lips right up against his ear so Bessie wouldn't hear me. "I hate you," I said, and then I wrapped my mouth around the spiny rim of his ear and bit it.

He hollered. The sleigh stopped, and for a moment, I felt triumphant.

When you have recently found out that your husband has betrayed you, those moments of triumph don't last long. Not to mention the thickening effects of morning sickness that eventually led me to the pharmacy, Bessie in tow, to the family planning aisle where she begged for one of the metallic, shiny, purple boxes of condoms, and I had to explain it wasn't full of candy. The next morning, with my human growth hormone-rich, first-morning urine, I peed into a cup and waited the requisite three minutes.

Afterward, I disposed of all the evidence in a plastic shopping bag. I took it straight out to the garbage bin while Bessie slept. It felt very possible to me that my life was over. I couldn't raise two children on my measly, part-time librarian's salary. I couldn't stay married to a man who screwed another woman, but showed the remorse of a swinger upon confession. And I couldn't hop down to my local abortion clinic for a vacuum job.

It was time for something to happen that I had long postponed: In the absence of Jeff, who was officially ousted from our home to a permanent conference, could I finally figure out if *I* had any thoughts of my own on the big issues of life? I couldn't go traveling across the world to figure this stuff out or write a memoir about it. I didn't have time or money to indulge. And I had Bessie; Bessie had only me. "When will Daddy come back?" she asked every ten seconds. I stopped listening. I started saying, "Isn't it fun just you and me together?"

Oh, it was fun all right, Mama: barfing in the morning, bitter by the afternoon. Marsha got me an afternoon at her favorite day spa, Lottie's.

"How is this going to help me figure things out?" I asked through a new onslaught of tears.

"It won't." She smiled and her eyes got lost in the soft folds of her face. "But your toes will look pretty when you're done."

Lottie Avery, proprietor of Lottie's, is a wild whirly-gig of a woman. Every time I saw her, she had different color hair. "Perk of the work," she said when I pointed it out. Lottie calls me "sugar doll." She calls everyone "sugar doll." She reminds me of some of the women in Atlanta, only she's not Southern. I don't know what she is. She paints her lips red. She took her real eyebrows off thirty years ago and draws new ones on each morning. She believes in cellulite cream. She believes it works. "I will make you beautiful," she claimed, brushing out my long, dark hair. When she stopped and put her hands on my head, she said, "The angels are speaking to me."

"What are they saying?" I asked Lottie.

"They say it will get better. They *promise* it will get better." And so I cried while she gave me a head massage, and I told her my husband, *Reverend* Winsted, slept with Lynn Periwynn, his ugly secretary.

"She's not so ugly, sugar doll," Lottie interrupted. "She's just never been loved enough to look pretty."

I carried on. I told her everything. I told her about the baby. She recommended I listen to the angels. When I told her I don't hear them, don't believe in them, don't believe in anything, she shook her head.

"Everyone believes in something," she scolded.

"I believe in evolution."

"Sugar doll," she said, shaking her head again, her almost white-blonde, heavily dyed head of short hair immobilized by hairspray. "You can't evolve your way out of this one."

When I left, she hugged me. "Trust the process," she said into my newly coiffed 'do.

"What would you do?" I asked.

"Now what does it matter what I'd do? Silly old lady like me." I frowned at her. "Trust the process, sugar doll. What else can you do?"

I could do a lot else, actually, it occurs to me as I drive home. For one thing, I could file for divorce. Armed with my freshly painted toenails, I arrive home, thank Marsha for babysitting, set Bessie in front of "Sesame Street," and began to research divorce attorneys. Later that night, after Bessie went to sleep, I put on the radio, drank a glass of wine, and danced around the kitchen, feeling — quite impossibly, it seemed — something like happy. It felt so good to have found a solution. A divorce, how perfectly simple! Now that I'd decided, a surge of joyful freedom ranged through me. Then Bob Marley's "Redemption Song" sang out from the Bose. "Emancipate yourself from mental slavery," he told me, melodically, urgently. Hadn't I done just that? I was going emancipate myself from *marital* slavery.

When I fell into bed at midnight, exhausted and exhilarated, I put a hand on my belly unthinkingly and remembered. How far along was I? I hadn't wanted to think of it. Could I be a single mother to two children? Was sleeping with Lynn a few times worth all the loss in Bessie's life, in my life?

You might as well have called me Sybil, because I plummeted like a roller coaster taking its greatest dive right down from my high into the pits of despair. I cried into my pillow like a fourteen-year-old who'd lost her first boyfriend. I cried so long, I lost track of time. I didn't get to sleep until after two. When Bessie woke me at six, curling up beside me, smelling like rising bread – that sweet, childhood smell – I broke again. *A baby*. I had to keep the family together.

I went later that day to the church to find Jeff. I didn't have much of a plan, only to find him, to reconcile with him, to move on. I figured the glory of the night before came partly out of hysteria and partly from wine. My new intention to keep the marriage alive grounded me. It made more sense. I was a big person, after all, I could overlook a minor infraction like this one, this "only a few times" kind of infidelity.

The church, a lovely white, New England edifice that plays home to a small, liberal congregation with a median age of sixty, smelled of popcorn when I walked in. Someone had made themselves a snack in the kitchen microwave. It occurred to me for the first time that I could very well run into Lynn. What would I say? What would I do? I would be dignified. I wouldn't hiss or spit or comment on her fat ankles or call her a home-wrecker. I would ignore her; that seemed like the best route. I wouldn't give her the benefit of my anger.

Standing at Jeff's office door, the rage I'd been feeling for weeks fell away. I'd stood at his door like that hundreds of times, ever since he took his position at Peaksville Church. It felt familiar and comforting and *normal* the way nothing had felt normal, since that sleigh ride. I put my hand on the doorknob. Why would I knock? He was *my* husband. I had never knocked before. We belonged to each other. We shared everything.

But the handle didn't budge. The office was locked. One of the trustees, Terrence Ranger, a man with a bushy beard and small, silvery blue eyes that always water, walked past me. He looked alarmed when he saw me. At first I feared for the worst; he *was* an old guy. Was he in pain? Having a stroke?

"Angie!"

"Terrence, are you okay?"

"I ought to be asking you that." He embraced me. I could smell the popcorn on him. When he pulled away, he said, "I am so sorry, Angie."

"You know?" This amazed and startled me. All that time, I didn't imagine anyone knowing, except Marsha, of course. And to have the entire church privy to my marriage's truly dirty underwear? I choked on a sob.

"Well, Jeff *did* have to tell us. For your sake. And Lynn's, of course."

I began to hyperventilate. "Lynn's sake?" I asked.

"How is Bessie taking it?"

"She misses him. She gets to see him four times a week, though."

"Between you and me," he said learning in so close, I could see the leftover popcorn skin in his teeth, "I think it's a terrible mistake."

"A mistake?" I asked, confused and now afraid.

"You can't build a partnership on an affair."

"No." I agreed with him, but what was I agreeing with? "I came to find Jeff. He always works Friday afternoons. I need to discuss a few things with him."

"Terrible." He shook his head. "It must be so hard for you."

"Yes, it is." I tried to nod amiably. I wanted him to leave. I wanted to find Jeff. "Do you know where Jeff has gone?" I didn't like it, not knowing the whereabouts of my own husband. I almost doubled over from the sick feeling in the pit of my stomach, and later, Terrence would retell the story and say I fainted *before* he spoke, and that if he hadn't been there to catch me, I would have banged my head on the corner of the brochure table stacked with pamphlets keen on the salvation of strangers.

"He and Lynn have gone together," he began, and *that's* when I fainted.

* * *

Later, Marsha would put Bessie down for the night, singing to her in a tender, sweet voice for upward of twenty minutes. I stood at the door, listening longingly. That's what

I loved about Marsha: her patience and quietude. For once, I didn't cry.

I told her everything, after she emerged from the dark, still room. I told her about waking up to Madeline Viver, the sexton, her pale doughy face staring ponderingly down at me. She was talking far too loudly. "You fainted!" she screamed in my direction. "Terrence came to find me! He thought it might be a female problem!"

Well, it certainly was a female problem. It was the kind of problem females had been having for generations: on the one hand, cheating spouse; on the other, pregnancy.

It alarmed Terrence and Madeline to discover that I had yet to be informed of Jeff and Lynn's vacation to Florida. Together. As a couple. And how did I not know that he had moved in with her? And the upcoming nuptials? They were only vague plans, Madeline assured me. No set date, but surely he'd bothered to inform me?

When I had finished reporting the ghastly news, Marsha did not speak. She didn't even seem to move. I listened to the hum of the standing lamp beside me. If I hadn't been in touch with my emotions before – and really I hadn't, I wasn't that kind of person; I didn't want to participate in the *process*, as Lottie would have said, of my own life—then I really didn't want to scratch below the surface. How had it come to this? Was Jeff so unhappy with me? Why hadn't I seen it coming? *Had* I seen it coming, and ignored it? Could I have done something different? Was he simply a bastard, a womanizing jerk?

The problem with Jeff-it-only-happened-a-few-times-Winsted running off with his church secretary for a prenuptial honeymoon – deserting his betrayed spouse in the freezing February New Hampshire cold – was not merely that now I could trust the certainty of his defection, but that I no longer had a choice in the matter. It didn't matter what I wanted to do, if I wanted to forgive him and move on, if I wanted to let go of the past and make the best of things. He'd made the decision for both of us. He and Lynn were the new family. And Bessie and I were alone.

I wasn't sure what to do, but I couldn't wait indefinitely. Every day I became more pregnant. Jeff called on his cell phone to say he couldn't pick up Bessie that week, but he didn't offer an explanation. I did not ask. I felt mute with rage and sorrow.

Marsha came with me to the clinic. She put on her stoic face. She would not give me her opinion. "Am I making a mistake?" I asked her, wringing my hands together in the waiting room.

"Some people think there are no mistakes."

"I don't know how I could do it. How would I pay for two children in daycare?"

"You could live with me," she said sweetly, placing a hand on my hands and squeezing them.

"I hate him so much," I said. "For ruining our family. For taking all of this away. What I'm really afraid of is not being able to love the baby. I'll have to share the baby with him. I'll have to see him more often. I will be more, not less, connected to him. Will he want the baby? Will he go to court and say that he and Lynn are better parents?"

I had been through all of these thoughts, all of them and more, day after agonizing day. I had a hard time laughing, even when Bessie would tickle my tickle spot at the bottom of my foot.

Marsha came into the room with me. She stood beside me. I had my feet in the stirrups. I felt obliterated by my situation. I hated Jeff, and on some level, the abortion felt like a punishment against him, which made no sense, of course, as I was the only one lying there. One of the nurses hummed the briefest few notes of a song, though enough that I could recognize the tune.

"What was that?" I asked, sitting up, so that the doctor sighed, tried to hide it. He was busy. He had people waiting. "What did you hum?"

The woman, younger than me and barely visible behind her scrub mask, half shrugged.

"*What* song did you just hum?" I asked more insistently. The young nurse shook her head.

"Well, tell her!" Marsha proclaimed, and though she's short and round and tends to wear large-print patterns and lacks all ferocity, this time she barked.

"You know," the nurse said, removing her mask. "That Bob Marley song." She hummed again.

"'Redemption Song,'" Marsha supplied. I looked at her, astonished. "I love reggae," she said simply.

I took my feet off the stirrups.

* * *

When Jeff showed up at my door, *our* door, some four months later, he stared agape at my belly. I didn't say a word and he began to cry. I invited him in. I gave him a cup of lemonade. He had not been to see us, to see Bessie, in all that time. He had been, all that time, in Florida. Terrence told me all this. He wanted me to know Jeff resigned from his position at Peaksville.

"Does he have another job?" I asked.

"We don't know," Terrence answered. "I think he couldn't face us."

"You deserve a better pastor," I told him.

Jeff did call during his Florida tenure, to talk to Bessie, and he did promise he would be back to see her soon. He rarely spoke more than a few words to me. One time, though, I asked him, "Are you happy now?"

"This is the worst time of my life," he answered. I laughed into the phone. Who was he kidding, off with Lynn, jobless and free in Florida like some college kid on a summer break. And there I was, lugging myself through the days, making a baby, taking care of another one, substituting at the elementary school to make extra cash outside of my library work, staying up well past midnight, sending out résumés. Who would take me on pregnant and give me an immediate maternity leave?

I had looked up "redemption" in the dictionary after Marsha brought me home from the women's clinic. It wasn't a word that had any real meaning to me, and I didn't like reggae. I hadn't even liked reggae in my twenties, when I should have because other people did. I didn't particularly like Bob Marley, and I had no idea what he was even saying in that song. I looked the lyrics up online. "Pirates? Atomic energy?" And yet, it hooked me, it spoke to me: It meant something I could not articulate, something that sit inside of me and grew, like the baby, only all mine.

"I can barely stand myself," I told Marsha. "My husband has run off with his homely secretary, and I've been saved by Bob Marley."

"I'll make fritters," she replied. "Eating will make you feel better."

And, in truth, eating did make me feel a little bit better. A lot of different things began to make me feel better; for one thing, moving out of the stage of morning sickness. For another, taking up some soul-searching. It had been so long since I'd given any thought to my own soul – whatever it is – that I'd nearly forgotten I even had one. Jeff had been the one to talk about redemption, in a religious way, about a redeemer. This still didn't make sense for me. It didn't work for me, and yet, I felt I had been redeemed, right on the table at the women's clinic, like I had been returned to myself. When I stood up and hopped off the table, I felt as though someone had given me back to myself. It took me weeks to understand a rising sense of gratitude toward Jeff, but eventually, I knew that I owed my new freedom to him. *He* had given me back to myself – by leaving.

What had happened in our marriage? I wasn't even sure, and I knew it wasn't his fault, but somehow, he got to be the good guy, the deep guy, the spiritual guy, the helpful one, the peaceful one, the joyful one. Day after day, without Jeff, I started to uncover myself. It was like reading a novel for the first time, turning the pages, threading out the plot.

I even came to see why Jeff had run off with Lynn: Although she wasn't pretty or fashionable or all that intelligent, no doubt she shared a whole system of belief with Jeff. They probably talked about their "walk with God," and she undoubtedly came with him each Sunday, as I never had, to church.

The day he showed up at my doorstep, I let him come in and sit at the kitchen table. Bessie rolled herself over him like a dog frolicking in animal crap. He wept openly. He begged my forgiveness. He wanted to tell me everything. He wanted to tell me he loved me. He wanted to tell me he'd left the church. He would never go back; it had ruined him, all that trying to be good, trying to be righteous. He wanted to tell me he wanted to be a farmer. He wanted me to know he hadn't seen Lynn in two months. His mistakes overwhelmed him. He was so sorry. Would I even consider?

Marsha made me a chocolate cake that night. We ate it after Jeff left, after Bessie fell asleep. She giggled as she decorated it, pressing out the tube of frosting to scrawl letters across the top.

"I call it my 'Risen from Florida' cake."

"What should I do?" I asked her as we ate it, piece after piece, the luscious, creamy center warm in our mouths.

"What do you want to do?"

"I don't know yet."

"Then wait." She smiled at me.

"Marsha, you're the best mother a girl could have."

"Some days, sweetheart, *you* are the reason I get out of bed. You and Bessie. And this one." She lightly touched my belly.

"You're lonely without Dad," I said.

"Well sure, sometimes. Will I sound trite if I tell you life is short?"

"You never sound trite. You are the definition of heart felt."

"Well, then, life is short." She smiled again. "And people die, sometimes too early."

When Jeff came back the next day, I sent Bessie off with Marsha to the farmers' market and my husband and I sat down to talk for the first time in years, it seemed. After that, he came to visit every day, for a few hours, until one night, Bessie and I invited him for dinner. That night, I let him stay until after sunset. I told him about the abortion, the almost-abortion. He cried again. "I don't deserve this," he said, looking at me and my belly and the house and toward Bessie's room.

"You're right," I told him. "None of us do. It's a gift. Isn't that what you tried to teach everyone?"

"I couldn't teach anybody anything. Not anymore. And I didn't know anything, even though I thought I did. All I know now is what I don't want to lose: you and Bessie."

Mmm. Well. I had to think about it. I took a meditation course. I refused to sleep with Jeff, refused to have him spend the night. He said all the right things, but I wasn't sure – not yet.

For months, he courted me. He worked to woo me back. I let him come to the birth. We both stared at Jason wide-eyed and amazed. That something so perfect, so wholly innocent and intact, could come out of our mess, not just the mess of us together, but each of our messes, and with such symmetry and harmony, two dark eyes gazing up. Jeff cried again. He cried in front of the nurses, in front of the doctor. "I am so lucky," he said.

In the middle of all this, in the midst of my slow return to clarity and sense and selfhood and mental freedom – the kind I decided Marley must have been singing about – my mother returned from Tibet and came to visit. I had not seen her in a decade. She told me all about her exciting adventures. She claimed she spent ten days in complete silence in a cave. When she asked if I missed her, I answered honestly.

"I don't know."

"Oh, Angela. You must be so hurt. Can you find it in your heart to forgive me? You'll *need* to forgive me. I've discovered, through my studies with the great masters, that forgiveness is the most healing power on Earth."

Later, not then, Jeff and I would laugh about this. We would laugh and laugh over the heads of our children at the irony and arrogance and ridiculousness of my mother, her hair slicked down close to her head, her skirt punctuated by tiny bells that rang every time she moved. We would hold our stomachs and cry, laughing at how silly she seemed – how presumptuous, how melodramatic – and it would connect us again. It would redeem us all over again, to one another, how funny it all was: the failing, the success. But then, I only smiled. I turned Jason over my shoulder for a burp.

"I agree," I said. "And sometimes, you don't even need a cave and a decade to learn what the monks and musicians all know. For some of us, all it takes is a sleigh ride."

Noche Buena

By Maria Geraci

Maggie Cartwright eyed the soggy fruitcake sitting in the backseat of her BMW. She shouldn't feel so giddy. Forty-eight-year-old women were not giddy. They were poised. Mature. Elegant. But Maggie didn't feel any of those. Especially not elegant. Not in this heat. She checked her lipstick in the car's rearview mirror. She had a pretty good inkling of how the fruitcake must feel. "How can I be sweating this much in December?" she muttered to herself.

Correction, said the voice in her head. *Ladies do not sweat, Margaret, they perspire.*

I have news for you, Ma. When you live in Old Explorers Bay, Florida, you sweat. Even on December 23rd, if the weather were so inclined.

Despite her wilted condition, she still looked pretty decent, didn't she? Of course, there were those tiny lines around her eyes. Nothing she could do about that. But the skin under her chin remained firm and her green eyes sparkled with excitement. She was a decade younger than

Christie Brinkley, and Christie Brinkley was still hot. At least to the over-forty crowd.

Maggie stepped carefully onto the asphalt. She was wearing four-inch heels with her standard holiday meet-and-greet attire: a no-sleeve, red-linen sheath and white, three-quarter-sleeve cashmere sweater and pearls (an outfit her mother would undoubtedly approve of). The heels were a concession to the otherwise June Cleaverish look expected of someone in her position. She leaned inside the car to pick up the fruitcake with both hands, straightened herself up, and with a forceful swing of her hip, slammed the car door shut.

North of Havana, the town's only Cuban restaurant, was the last trip on Maggie's "Goodwill Tour of the Fruitcakes." Every December 23rd, a representative of the *Daughters of the Spanish Explorers* (the town's most prominent women's club) brought a fruitcake and a Christmas card to all the local merchants. This year, as the club's secretary, the task had fallen on Maggie. She'd purposely kept North of Havana as her last stop. It had given her something to look forward to.

The smell of simmering pork and *sofrito* made Maggie's mouth water. She scanned the empty dining room with its scrubbed down Formica tables and brightly colored walls with the mural scenes of old Havana's *Malecón*. Nestor had painted those murals himself.

She would never forget the first time she laid eyes on Nestor Vega. It was two years ago that she'd taken Lily, her Bison Frise, for her nightly stroll through down town when she'd spotted the lights in the abandoned restaurant building. Greg, Maggie's brother-in-law and president of the First Coast Bank and Trust, had mentioned someone had bought the building, but he hadn't given her details. As a past president of the Chamber of Commerce, Maggie's curiosity had been aroused. She had put on her best "welcome to Old Explorers Bay" smile and prepared to greet the newest member of the business community, the Cuban immigrant from Miami who'd moved to Old Explorer's Bay to open his own restaurant.

Faded jeans. No shirt. No shoes. Standing on a ladder and painting the restaurant walls fast and furiously to the sounds of Celia Cruz blaring from a portable CD player. Nestor, with his rough good looks and suave voice with the accent. He was Javier Bardem and Antonio Banderas wrapped up like the finest tobacco leaves to form the perfect Cuban cigar.

"Please don't tell me you're on fruitcake duty this year." Nestor's deep voice sent a scratchy thrill up Maggie's spine.

She turned to see him standing outside the kitchen doorway. "No customers today?"

"The last one just left. I'm closing early. Tomorrow is *Noche Buena.*"

"*Noche Buena*?"

"Christmas Eve," he said.

"I thought *Noche Buena* meant goodnight."

"That's *buenas noches*." He nodded at the fruitcake. "So, I take it that's for me?"

"Baked *especially* for you and the rest of the good merchants of Old Explorer's Bay." Maggie paused for dramatic effect. "By Ellen Tucker."

Nestor flinched.

Ellen Tucker was the worst cook in the club. But she always insisted on making her traditional holiday fruitcake, and no one had the heart to dissuade her.

"I thought we were friends," Nestor said, his dark eyes shining with humor. He took the fruitcake and placed it on the counter next to the cash register. "I suppose this is the part where I say 'thank you.'"

"It is. And, you're welcome." Now that she'd delivered the cake, there was no real reason to linger. She still had her own holiday baking to do and last-minute presents to wrap and a thousand other tiny details to take care of, but she couldn't bring herself to leave just yet. "So are you closed all through the holidays?" The question she really wanted to ask was whether or not Nestor was leaving town. Maggie knew he had cousins in Miami. Is that where he was spending Christmas?

"Just the next two days. I thought I'd relax. Do a little fishing, maybe. I'll be open again for business on the 26th. You should stop by. I'm making *boliche*."

So Nestor wasn't leaving town.

"Maybe I will," she said. "Turkey leftovers have never been my favorite."

Nestor crossed his arms over his chest and leaned back against the counter. "What is your favorite? Food, that is?"

Without hesitating, Maggie replied, "Italian. Pasta, mostly."

"Then, why don't you have that for Christmas?"

Maggie blinked. "Because it's not traditional. We always have turkey for Christmas dinner."

"But you don't like it?"

"My mother's turkey is too dry. And she always insists we sit in the formal dining room, all dressed up in our Christmas sweaters. No matter how warm it might be outside." She shrugged. "You know Florida Christmases: One year, it might be freezing cold; another year you have to have the air conditioning on just to get through the day."

Nestor nodded. "Very much like Christmas back in Cuba. Although we didn't have an air conditioner."

Despite their two-year friendship, they rarely spoke of each other's pasts. Maggie knew Nestor had been born in Cuba and had spent his childhood and teen years on the communist island under Castro's regime. He had come to America in 1980 during the large influx of immigrants known as "*marielitos*." He'd worked in restaurants all his life and had saved for years to open his own place. He was fifty years old, married briefly and divorced. No children. He liked baseball and had his own boat. He could make a mean *ropa vieja,* was friendly to everyone and didn't mind when Maggie brought Lily into the restaurant on her nightly walk through town. It was those times while Maggie sipped on a *cortadito* with Lily in her lap, talking to Nestor about the events of the day, that she thought there was some spark of attraction between them. On her side, definitely. But although Nestor sometimes flirted with her, nothing ever came of it. Shanna Davis, who worked at the post office, had asked Nestor out once, but according to her, he had gently turned her down. As far as Maggie knew he hadn't dated anyone since moving to town.

Since he brought up the subject, she decided to probe a bit. "What was Christmas like back in Cuba?"

"Back then, Christmas was like any other day. We worked or went to school. But my *abuela* always tried to make a *lechon*. There was no money for presents, so after dinner, we played cards or dominos. Went for a swim in the ocean if it wasn't too chilly. What about you?"

"When I was a girl, we went to my grandfather's cabin in Tennessee. It was always cold, but some years, if we were lucky, it snowed. My sister and brother and I had snowball fights. We went to church, ate some of my mom's dry turkey and too much of the pecan pie. That sort of thing." There had been presents, too. Lots of them. But after hearing Nestor's version of Christmas, she decided to omit that part.

"I've never seen snow, but it sounds like fun."

"You've *never* seen snow?"

"Not much snow in Havana. Or Florida, either," he said.

Maggie felt herself flush. She was always making these kinds of stupid comments around Nestor. He must think her the biggest ninny in the world.

"Tell me more about your Christmas in Tennessee," he urged. "There must have been presents. What was your favorite?"

"Actually," she said, "my favorite present was the cardboard box my sister Nora's dollhouse came in."

Nestor shook his head. "A cardboard box?"

"One year, Nora got this huge dollhouse from Santa," Maggie explained, smiling at the memory. "My brother found the cardboard box it had come in and he made it into a makeshift sleigh. My sister and I took turns riding it while he pulled us. We played on that sleigh for hours. I always thought ... well, I always thought I'd bring my own kids up to the cabin. Do a repeat of the things Dan and Nora and I used to do."

"Why didn't you have children?" Nestor asked.

Coming from anyone else, the question might have seemed rude or too personal, but Maggie could tell Nestor was genuinely interested.

"My husband died before we got around to it," Maggie said. *Among other things.*

Nestor nodded thoughtfully. "Jack Cartwright. He was an attorney, wasn't he?"

Maggie was surprised that he knew even that small tidbit about Jack. She'd spoken about her late husband to Nestor a few times, but she didn't remember telling him what Jack had done for a living. "That's right."

"And a property owner."

"Jack's family used to own half this town." As a result, Maggie was probably the richest person in Old Explorers Bay. It was both a boon and a curse. She enjoyed living a good life, and she liked giving back to the community whenever she could, but being Jack Cartwright's widow also meant she did things like deliver fruitcakes two days before Christmas.

"You must have loved him very much to have never remarried."

"Something like that," she said.

Nestor must have read the discomfort in her voice. He looked at her with the same pity everyone else in Old Explorers Bay did whenever they talked about Jack. She could take it from everyone else, but not from Nestor Vega.

She forged up her best Chamber of Commerce smile. "I've kept you long enough. Gotta go! Have a very Merry Christmas, Nestor!"

She was almost out the door, when she heard him answer quietly. "You too, Maggie."

* * *

Maggie had just let Lily out of her kennel when her cell phone rang. She thought about ignoring it but if she didn't pick up immediately, her mother would just keep calling anyway. "Hey, Mom. What's up?"

"I wanted to make sure you were bringing the pecan pies to Christmas dinner."

"Of course I'm bringing the pies. Don't I always?" Maggie tried not to sound impatient. Her mother was seventy-six years old. Still energetic enough to make her annual, five-course Christmas dinner, and still prickly enough to nag everyone involved with it. Christmas dinner was a family tradition that no one dared alter. Her sister, Nora, made her famous, super-secret stuffed mushroom caps as appetizers (although they all knew the recipe was really Paula Dean's);

her sister-in-law, Josie, brought the mashed potatoes (always lumpy, but everyone pretended not to notice); and Maggie brought the pies. Her mother cooked everything else herself, mostly because she didn't trust anyone else to do it right.

"It doesn't hurt to check that you're on track with your baking. Remember, the Piggly Wiggly will be closing early tomorrow. If you don't have all the ingredients by now --"

"I have all the ingredients."

"Did you know that Alice is bringing a boyfriend? I hope the weather turns cool enough that everyone can wear their holiday sweaters. I just *hate* serving Christmas dinner to a bunch of people in shorts. Alice wouldn't date anyone who wore shorts at the Christmas table, would she?"

Alice was Nora's oldest daughter, home for the holidays from her junior year at the University of Florida.

"I have no idea, Mom. What does Nora think of the boyfriend?"

"Nice enough, I suppose. From south Florida, though." There was a tick of disdain in her mother's voice. It only lasted a second. "It makes an even dozen for dinner, which is wonderful, because now I can use the whole table. I can't remember the last time I used all twelve settings of my china. Oh, well, I mean ... of course I *remember*. It's when Jack was still alive." Her mother had adored Jack Cartwright.

Sometimes, Maggie thought her mother missed Jack more than Maggie did.

Correction: Her mother *definitely* missed Jack more. How depressing was that?

"What if I invited someone to dinner? Do you think we can squeeze in thirteen?"

"Who would you bring to Christmas dinner?"

"Someone who doesn't have anywhere else to go?"

"No family? Not at Christmas?"

"Not any in town."

There was an inelegant pause. "I only have twelve settings of the Limoges. I suppose I could mix and match with something else, but it would look so shabby. Who are you inviting?"

Not enough settings for the table? Whatever happened to peace and goodwill toward all men? Maggie had a sudden need to shock her mother into the Yuletide spirit. "I'm bringing my boyfriend," she said.

Her mother laughed. "Oh, Maggie, I thought you were being serious!"

"I am serious. What if I told you I had a boyfriend?"

"You're almost fifty years old. What do you want with a boyfriend?"

"I'm forty-eight and if I have to tell you what I want with a boyfriend, then I think the past thirty years must have been pretty crummy for Dad."

"All right, then. Who is this boyfriend? What's his name?"

"His name is ... okay, there is no boyfriend," she admitted.

"That's what I thought." She could almost hear her mother shaking her head through the phone line. "Maggie, what's gotten into you? Lately, you seem so ... restless."

Ladies are not restless, Margaret. They are tranquil, cool, calm ...

"I was thinking of inviting Nestor Vega to dinner."

"Isn't he that Puerto Rican who owns the Latino diner on Main Street? The one who looks like he's had his nose broken in a street fight?"

"Nestor is Cuban, not Puerto Rican."

"Isn't it the same thing?"

"No, Mom, it isn't."

"I'm just not sure. I mean, if Alice hadn't invited her young man, then of course, we'd still have enough room at the table --"

"Just forget it," Maggie interrupted. "It was a stupid idea, anyway."

"Maybe we can invite this Nestor person some other time. Do his people celebrate Thanksgiving?"

"Thanksgiving was last month."

"I mean for next year."

Maggie felt like her head was going to explode. "He's lived in this country for over thirty years, so yeah, I'm pretty sure he celebrates everything we do."

"Well! There you go. I'll put him on the calendar for next Thanksgiving."

If Alice's boyfriend didn't become a permanent fixture at their holiday table, that is. "Sure, sounds great, Mom."

* * *

Maggie took the last of the pecan pies out of the oven and placed it on the kitchen counter. She closed the window above the sink, afraid the nippy air might cool them off too quickly. Sometime in the middle of the night, the temperature had dropped. Al Roker was predicting a white Christmas for half the nation. Her mother was probably doing the happy dance. No shorts for tomorrow night's dinner. They could all wear their Christmas sweaters while sitting at the table with the Limoges china. All twelve settings. The world was back on track.

There was a knock at the kitchen door. Her sister.

"Smells yummy," said Nora.

"I hear Alice has a boyfriend."

Nora broke off a piece of the crust from one of the pies. Maggie tried to stop her, but she was too fast. "His name is John Edward Beckett, the third. But he goes by Skip."

"Wow. With a name like that, I'm sure Mom would let him get away with shorts at the Christmas table."

"What?" Nora asked, munching on piecrust.

"Never mind," said Maggie. "Hey, Nora, when was the last time you were at Grandpa's cabin?"

Nora scrunched her face in thought. "Must be a couple of years ago, when the kids were still all going to camp for the summer. Why?"

Because ever since her conversation with Nestor, Maggie hadn't been able to get the cabin out of her mind. It would do her good to get away for a few weeks. Re-evaluate her life, maybe.

"I've been thinking about driving up there after the holidays. Is it still in good shape?" Maggie asked.

"There's a company that oversees the maintenance, so yeah, I think so." Nora snatched another edge of the piecrust. At this rate, it might just be better to trim the whole crust off. Or start over and bake another pie, which Maggie wasn't in the mood for. "What are you going to do up there?"

"I don't know. Paint. Read. Sleep." *Think about how empty my life is and what I can do to get it back on track.*

"All by yourself?"

"Of course not all by myself. I'll take Lily."

Nora appeared to let that sink in.

"What are you doing here, anyway?" Maggie asked. "It's barely eight a.m."

"Mom called last night. She wants you to bring the pies over today so she can make sure they're done, only she didn't want to ask you herself on account of you being in a weird mood."

"Who said I was in a weird mood?"

"Mom. She's worried about you."

"It sounds like she's more worried about the pies."

Nora's expression turned serious. "Did you know that Nestor Vega was in prison?"

Maggie stilled. "Who told you that?"

"Greg. It came up when Nestor got his loan for the restaurant."

"When? Where? For what?"

"Greg wouldn't tell me any of the details. Privileged customer information and all that." Nora eyed her speculatively. "Mom is afraid you're sleeping with Scarface."

"*What*?"

"You know, that movie about the Cuban refugee who became the Godfather of Miami? Al Pacino was in it. And Michelle Pfeiffer ... but I can't remember if it was before or after she was in 'Grease 2,' which was perfectly awful, if you ask me."

Maggie had read an article once about the *Marielitos*. Castro had literally opened the gates to Cuba's prisons and insane asylums, and dumped his most unwanted citizens on Florida's shore. Nestor certainly wasn't crazy. And Maggie found it impossible to believe sweet, friendly Nestor could have done anything to land him in prison. Al Pacino's character had been a *Marielito*, but *no way* was Nestor anything like the thug Pacino had portrayed.

Nora frowned. "Of course, personally I don't think Nestor would have gotten a loan at the First Coast Bank and Trust if he'd killed anyone or robbed a bank or anything *too* violent. Maybe he went to jail for being a deadbeat dad or not paying his taxes or something."

"Oh, for the love of God! I'm *not* sleeping with Nestor Vega!"

"Too bad," said Nora. She reached out and broke off another piece of piecrust and shoved it in her mouth. "Because if there's anyone in this town that a woman like you should sleep with, then it's definitely Nestor Vega."

"What do you mean, a woman like me?" Maggie demanded, not caring at this moment if Nora wanted to wolf down an entire pie.

"You know, repressed."

"I'm *not* repressed."

"When was the last time you had sex?"

Maggie's shoulders slumped. If frequency of sex was Nora's measuring stick for repression, then Maggie was definitely repressed.

"And please don't tell me it was with Jack," said Nora. "Jack died ten years ago."

Maggie tightened her jaw.

Her sister's eyes widened. "Oh! I thought ... well, I thought maybe you'd managed to get a little somethin' somethin' on the sly, you know?"

"In this town?"

Nora gave her the same pitying look that Nestor had given Maggie yesterday. "So the pies are good to go and you're not going to end up like Michelle Pfeiffer in *Scarface*. My work here is done," she said.

"I'll make a point to tell Mom how you straightened me out. You'll still be her special girl."

"Damn right, I am. I work hard for that title. Listen, I'd stay longer and chat, but I have to drop by the Piggly Wiggly to get the ingredients for my super-secret stuffed mushroom caps so I can make them at the last minute. See you tomorrow!"

Nora was gone a full five minutes before Maggie was able to think clearly again.

Nestor Vega had been in prison?

* * *

Maggie pulled her shoulder-length hair back in a low ponytail, grabbed an old sweater from the back of her closet, and loaded Lily and the pecan pies into the car. It was nippier than Maggie had thought, probably in the mid-forties, which was freezing by north-Florida standards. Her jeans had holes in the knees (bought that way on purpose) and Maggie should probably change into a nicer pair. But the hell with it: If her mother gave her any flak about them Maggie would just use it as an excuse to get away early.

She pulled out of the garage and pushed the button above the car visor that automatically shut the door. The five-thousand-square-foot house was a showcase, glittering with the traditional decorations. "All dressed up and nowhere to go," she muttered to the house. It was silly, still holding onto it. Not that she couldn't afford it, but all that emptiness ... Funny enough, it had never bothered her before. After Jack died, she'd kept busy. She'd been Chamber of Commerce president for three years and had been on the committee to bring new business to town. She'd traveled and babysat for her nieces and nephews. She belonged to two book clubs, a cooking club and a tennis team. She had even run the Boston Marathon a few years ago. She had a full, productive life.

But she hadn't lied to Nora: There'd been no one since Jack.

Not that a few of the locals hadn't tried to wine and dine her at first. But her lack of interest had been duly noted. And then she'd turned forty, and the men available hadn't exactly been the cream of the crop. None of that had mattered, though. Not until a couple of years ago. Her mother was right: She was restless.

Maggie took a detour through Main Street. Old Explorers Bay was a small town, even by north Florida's standards. Nestled just a few miles south of St. Augustine, it had all the beauty of the nation's oldest city, but not the huge tourist crowds. Still, they didn't do half-bad, Maggie thought proudly. There were six bed-and-breakfast inns (usually always booked), three seafood restaurants, an old-time coffee shop, a bakery and Nestor's restaurant.

Speaking of which ...

The lights were on in North of Havana. Strange, considering that Nestor had told her he'd be closed Christmas Eve.

She parked her car in front of the restaurant and pulled Lily into her arms. Through the glass exterior, she could see Nestor, high up on a ladder, paintbrush in hand. Maggie tested the restaurant door. It was unlocked. Nestor hadn't seen her yet. He was engrossed in his painting, and she didn't want to startle him by her sudden appearance. But she wasn't going to leave without speaking to him.

She eased herself through the door and silently watched as he angled his paintbrush to add small touches to what she thought was an already perfect mural. There was no Celia Cruz in the background this time. He was listening to Tom Petty and he was fully clothed: jeans, sneakers and a paint-stained sweatshirt. Maggie felt a wave of lust take her down. She must have made a sound, because he turned to face her.

"Maggie!" he said with a grin. He climbed down from the ladder and wiped his hands on his sweatshirt. "What are you doing here?"

"I thought you were going fishing."

He walked over and nuzzled Lily's ears. "Too cold," he said with a shrug. He eyed her jeans with the torn knees. "Where were you heading?"

To my mother's. To bring her the pecan pies for tomorrow's utterly boring and awful Christmas dinner.

She thought about the pitying looks Nestor had given her the day before. And the similar look her sister had given her that morning. But Maggie didn't want anyone's pity. She wanted ... well, she wasn't sure what she wanted, but she definitely knew what she didn't want. And that was spending tomorrow sitting at her mother's perfectly laid table with the

Limoges china, making small talk to Alice's boyfriend, Skip, from south Florida.

"I'm going to my grandfather's cabin in Tennessee. I want to see snow again. Do you want to come with me?" Her voice sounded oddly husky and far away, like she was listening to herself talk on a mic.

Nestor raised a dark brow.

"I know it sounds crazy and it's short notice," she said. "I'm supposed to be on my way to my mother's to deliver the Christmas pies. Plus, I don't have any extra clothes with me, but you said you'd never seen snow and I thought --"

"Yes," he interrupted.

"Yes?" she squeaked.

Nestor replaced the lid on the can of paint and tossed the paintbrush into a sink full of murky looking water. "Yes, let's go. Now."

"Okay," Maggie said. Out of the corner of her eye, she saw him grab the fruitcake off the counter. She was too dazed to protest.

* * *

They were almost to Savannah when Maggie thought to call her mother. They had stopped to fill the car with gas, and Nestor had taken over driving. She pulled out her cell phone, punched in the number, and then changed her mind. She turned her phone off and stuck it back in the bottom of her purse. "I should probably call my mom and tell her where I am," said Maggie.

"So why don't you?" Nestor asked.

"I'll call her later." Traffic was easing off. Maggie fidgeted nervously in her seat. What was she doing? She was in a car with Nestor Vega on her way to Tennessee! And she hadn't told anyone. Not her mother. Not her sister ...

"Is there something wrong?" Nestor asked.

It was a nine-hour-plus drive to the cabin. She might as well get it over with. "My sister told me you were in prison. Is it true?" she asked.

Nestor didn't hesitate. "Yes."

She waited for him to elaborate, but he didn't. "You don't have to tell me about it. If you don't want to, that is."

"You knew I'd been in prison, but you still got in a car with me. Alone?"

"Well ... there is Lily. She might look like a worthless ball of fluff, but she's been trained to bite first, ask questions later."

Nestor smiled.

Maggie took a deep breath and slowly let it out. "My husband cheated on me. With just about every single woman in town. Some married ones, too. He said it didn't mean anything. That he loved me and that it would never happen again. But it always did."

Nestor's smile faded.

"I never had children, because I didn't want to. Not with Jack. I was on the verge of filing for divorce when he had his accident." Maggie shrugged. "Believe it or not, for a long time, I actually felt guilty about it."

"And that's why you never remarried? Because you think all men are cheaters?"

"I've had enough therapy to know that isn't true. Jack's cheating was about Jack and his own insecurities. It had nothing to do with me. Except that maybe I can be an enabler for bad behavior. I've never remarried, because there hasn't been anyone I've been interested in dating. Until you came to town, that is."

Nestor's gaze jerked off the road to stare at her.

"Please don't get us killed on Christmas Eve," Maggie joked.

He turned his attention back to the road. "Maggie --"

"You don't have to say anything," she rushed. "I just wanted you to know how I felt. We're friends, and I don't want to mess that up." Before he could respond, she reached into her purse and pulled out her cell phone.

Her mother answered on the first ring. "Where are you? Your sister said you were going to stop by and deliver the pies."

"I'm on my way to Tennessee."

"Oh, Maggie! Stop teasing."

"I'm being perfectly serious. I'm on my way to the cabin. But don't worry, I'm not alone, Mother. Lily and Nestor are with me. Oh, and we have one fruitcake and two pecan pies. Well, not exactly. We have one fruitcake and three quarters pie left, because we already ate some."

Silence.

"Mom, are you still there?"

"This is a very childish prank, Maggie, but if you insist on having your way, then very well. By all means, invite this Nestor Vega person to dinner. I think Nora's china has a similar look to my Limoges. We can use that at the table. Now. Are you happy?"

Maggie glanced over at Nestor, who was diligently keeping his eyes straight ahead on the road as requested.

"Yes, Mother, I think I am happy."

Nestor glanced cautiously in her direction.

"Deliriously happy," Maggie continued. "Because I'm on my way to Tennessee with Nestor."

"This isn't a joke, is it?"

"No, it's no joke. You're the one who always reminding me that I'm almost fifty years old, so I thought I better start acting like it. I'm spending my Christmas with Nestor and Lily at the cabin. I'm sorry about the pies. I should have dropped them off at the house, but I was too caught up in the moment to think clearly. But don't worry: If you hurry, you can probably get to the Piggly Wiggly before they close. I'm sure they still have a few premade pies left in the bakery."

* * *

They had just crossed the Tennessee border when they saw the first snow flurries. It was almost dusk, but there was still enough light to catch the tiny bits of white fluff that dropped from the sky. Nestor was like a kid, pointing to each and every one, occasionally laughing and making small talk, but Maggie still felt an inkling of discomfort from their earlier conversation.

It wasn't that she was sorry she'd told Nestor how she felt about him. It was just that despite her protest to the contrary, she'd hoped for something more than just friendship. Of course, she'd stopped him before he could respond to her amorous confession. Why had she done that?

Maggie gripped the wheel and began the slow incline up the mountain. Nestor had driven for almost six hours straight, and Maggie had had to insist it was her turn to drive. After what seemed like an eternity up a two-lane mountain road, they reached Gatlinburg. The town looked like something from a Christmas postcard with twinkling lights and decorations everywhere. Tourists jammed the sidewalks, crossing the streets willy nilly without bothering to worry about the bumper-to-bumper traffic. It took almost an hour to get to the other side of town and begin their ascent up yet another mountain. By the time they reached the cabin, Maggie was both mentally and physically exhausted. At the higher elevation, there was snow everywhere. Maggie's heart began to beat furiously. She didn't know whether it was from excitement or nervousness. Or both.

She parked the car and opened the door to let Lily out.

Nestor took one look at her grandfather's mountain retreat and shook his head. "I thought you said this was a cabin."

"It is. Sort of."

"More like a mansion," Nestor said. But he didn't seem prickly about it. More resigned than anything, and Maggie wondered for the first time if Nestor was one of those men who had a problem with women who had more money than they did. But there was nothing she could do about that. She'd accepted Nestor for who he was. If there was any future for their friendship, he'd have to do the same for her.

She walked around to the side of the house to the woodpile and reached around to find the small, tin box where they kept a spare key. Much to her relief, the key was still there. It had occurred to her on the drive up the mountain that maybe it would be missing, in which case she wasn't sure what they would do. Luckily, it wasn't an issue.

Nestor picked up a load of wood and followed her into the house. Maggie flipped on the lights. The house was so cold, she could see her own breath.

"The sooner we get a fire going, the better," Nestor said. He didn't meet her gaze or say anything else.

Maggie checked the thermostat and turned on the heat. There were four bedrooms, all with their own baths. Despite having almost all day to think about what they were doing, it occurred to her that she hadn't really thought anything through at all. They had no spare clothes, no personal toiletries, no food, nothing. Just themselves, one almost inedible fruitcake and one pecan pie left. It was two hours till Christmas. Nothing would be open for a couple of days.

She cleared her throat to get Nestor's attention. "There's a bedroom upstairs you can use. There should be plenty of blankets and stuff like that. I'm just going to freshen up. In the bedroom. Down here," she emphasized.

She thought she saw Nestor smile.

God. She felt herself turn red. What where they doing? Had this been a mistake? It occurred to her that the reason she'd cut Nestor off earlier was because she didn't want to hear the same polite brush-off he'd given Shanna Adams. She'd rather not hear anything.

She found clean towels and soap in the bathroom linen closet, as well as a couple of old jackets and one pair of mittens. They could take turns wearing the mittens, or maybe they could wear one each. She headed back to the living room to show Nestor her find, but he wasn't there. A burgeoning fire crackled in the grate. Maggie rubbed her hands near the flames. Nestor must have followed her lead and gone upstairs to freshen up.

Lily began to bark. She ran to the door, her tail wagging. Was there someone outside? Maggie opened the door to find Nestor grinning at her.

"Are you ready?" he asked.

"For what?"

He took her by the hand and led her to the side of the house, where the snow-covered yard gently sloped to form a small hill. A large, plastic garbage can lid with a piece of rope tied to one end lay on the snow. "I couldn't find any cardboard in the garage, so I made do with what you had." He picked Lily up in his arms. "Get in," he urged.

Maggie was too surprised to protest. She gingerly lowered herself onto the lid. Nestor placed Lily in Maggie's arms. "Hold on," he said.

Maggie barely had time to do just that before Nestor grabbed the other end of the rope and began running down the hill. The wind whipped her ponytail back and stung her eyes. Lily barked playfully, and Maggie could hear herself laugh. They reached the end of the slope, but Nestor kept running, his sneakers crunching (and most likely getting soaked) in the snow. He must have run for almost half a mile before he collapsed on the snow-covered ground. The sudden jerking stop made Maggie roll out of the lid and onto the snow next to Nestor. Lily jumped in the air and began running in circles around them.

"Oh, Nestor! That was wonderful," said Maggie.

He reached out and pulled her into his arms. Maggie froze, but despite the chilly temperature and the sudden dampness, she could feel creeping through her jeans, she felt hot all over. Nestor was going to kiss her. And she was going to let him. Hell, she was going to do more than just let him: She was going to kiss him back.

"I went to prison twice," said Nestor. "The first time when I was fourteen. For stealing food. The second time I went for protesting against the government. They called it 'insurrection.' I was sixteen then and probably would have rotted there if Castro hadn't decided to flush his toilets into the United States. I have my GED, but I've never been to college – never been much of anywhere, really. The only money I have is what I've invested in the restaurant. I work twelve, sometimes fourteen hours a day, six days a week." He paused. "I'm not much of a catch, Maggie. But I can tell you this: I would never cheat on you."

Maggie gulped in a lungful of cold mountain air. "I know that."

"How?" asked Nestor. "How can you possibly know that about me?"

"I don't know. I just do," said Maggie. "Maybe it's because of all the little things. Like the way you watch for me through the restaurant window every night when I take Lily for a walk. Or the way you remember exactly the way I like my *cortadito*. Or the incredible amount of detail you put into painting those murals that remind you of your birthplace. Or ... even just this. This sleigh ride, which, believe me, is something I'll remember for the rest of my life."

He kissed her then, and Maggie thought he whispered something about this being the best *Noche Buena* he'd ever had, and Maggie had to agree. It wasn't until they were on their way back to the cabin, holding hands that Maggie thought to ask him the question burning in her brain.

"By the way, what are you doing next Thanksgiving?"

Fairy Lights

By Jenny Peterson

Allison burrowed deeper into her oversized parka and snuck a glance at her little sister. They were sitting close in the small, wooden sleigh, but the cold distance between them felt like miles.

Willow had walked off the plane three days ago completely unprepared for the snapping cold of northern Sweden: a thin scarf draped around her neck and tall, brown boots pulled up over her dark jeans. They had hugged and Allison had made some exclamations about how excited she was to finally see Willow, then they had fallen into an awkward silence.

"So, Dad's good?" Allison had asked for the second time. She had kept her eyes on the road as she said it, threading the all-terrain truck she'd borrowed from her anthropology professor along the narrow strip of asphalt that lead to the indigenous, Sami settlement where she'd lived for the past two years.

Willow had shrugged and bit at a short nail, the midnight blue polish chipped at the tips. "In Hilton Head for the holidays with *Miranda*." She said the name with disgust, like it felt dirty in her mouth. Miranda. Their dad's new wife. "Sorry I didn't come back for their wedding," Allison had said.

Willow shrugged again and looked out the window, her shoulders hunched. "Why would you?"

The harsh tone of her little sister's voice stung, and Allison frowned. She didn't have an answer, not a good one at least. She was thrown off-kilter, like she was trying to stand in a canoe, by the quiet anger in her sister's voice. She had wanted to go home for the wedding, a small beach ceremony that looked lovely from the photos their dad and Miranda had brought with them when they'd visited not long after. She had wanted to go, but that would mean ...

"And ... and Mom?" Allison had asked quietly, thinking of the woman who was the reason she stayed away.

Willow, if she had heard her, didn't respond. She had kept her eyes trained on the window and hunched a little more.

This far north, the sun was almost a memory at this time of the year, only making a fleeting trip across the sky before the ever-present night returned. In the falling darkness, Allison could see her reflection against the window: pallid skin, pale blue eyes, blonde hair. Even the long scar that slashed down her cheek had faded to a light pink. A friend had once told her she looked like a delicate china doll, but Allison was more inclined to think she looked like all color had leached away from her.

Beside her, Willow was warmer. Her matching blonde hair—their mother's hair—framed fair skin splashed with light freckles and expressive brown eyes. Or, at least, that was what she had looked like two years ago when Allison had left. Her sister's brown eyes, Allison had noticed as they'd hugged briefly in the entrance of the small airport, were dull and hard. She had told herself it was jetlag.

Allison looked through her reflection as she drove ever north. It was too dark to see much beyond the glow of the headlights, but she didn't need daylight to picture the landscape of northern Sweden, the vast expanse of snow and ice all around, only broken by the glimpse of deep green that peeked from snow-bent pines and the craggy, gray peaks that sawed across the horizon like jagged teeth. There was something in the silent isolation of this sparse, untamed wilderness that Allison had come to love in the years she'd lived with the Sami people and studied their lives, but she had become suddenly unsure if Willow would feel the same as they drove silently through the snow.

Allison had never been spectacular at small talk, but that had never been a problem when it came to bubbly, talkative Willow. But, Allison reminded herself, her sister had been 12 the last time she'd seen her — the day she'd finally left. A 14-year-old girl was an entirely different creature.

Three days into the visit, Allison was still unsure what Willow thought of her home, of anything about the new life she had made for herself. It hurt to see her little sister like this, withdrawn into a hard shell that reminded Allison too much of the woman she'd run from two years ago. Willow was all angles now — sharp cheekbones that made the shadows under her eyes seem like bruises and long, bony limbs that she folded into herself. The silence over the past three days had been thick and uncomfortable; Willow filling the small cottage with a black mood that Allison didn't know how to lift.

On a sleigh ride that Allison had planned weeks ago —an activity that now seemed laughably naïve and pointless — Allison pressed her lips together as she peeked at Willow. Her blonde hair spilled out from under the borrowed hat and her upturned nose was red with cold, nestled against the purple scarf.

Allison nudged her sister, their matching puffy parkas scratching like vinyl where they rubbed together.

"Pretty, isn't it?"

They were riding in the snug seat of the sleigh, two massive reindeer pulling them through the dense pines, their deep-green boughs sagging under the weight of snow like heavy whipped cream. Above, a million shades of white glittered and winked against the velvet blue sky.

Willow shrugged, her thin shoulders barely making the oversized jacket move, and tucked her nose into the scarf. "Freezing, more like."

"You'll get used to it. It's at least better than August at home when Mom refuses to turn on the A/C," Allison said, remembering all too well the sticky days in eastern Ohio when the air was so thick she felt like she was breathing in soup. She felt strange talking about their mom, someone she'd avoided mentioning for years now, but she didn't know what else to talk about with Willow. It seemed their tenuous connection through family was now the only relationship they had. It made a harsh bark of laughter rise in the back of her throat to think *that* was the person she'd bring up to try and get any response out of her sister.

"How would you know," Willow muttered, barely audible against the muffle of the scarf. "You don't live there anymore."

Allison frowned, but didn't respond. Instead, she turned away and busied herself pulling a big blanket onto their laps, the thick weave heavy on her legs.

In the silence, Allison could hear the creak of the pines and the whisper of the sleigh as it glided through the fluff of deep snow. The reindeer snorted and puffed as they pulled, mist from their warm breath pushing whorls of white into the air, and the bells around their necks sending muted echoes through the silent, midnight world of northern Sweden.

The snow and sleigh reminded Allison so much of home, of their cabin in northern Michigan where she had taught Willow how to build a snow fort. She had helped her sister's hands—made clumsy by thick mittens and layers of clothing—form snowballs, and shouted with laughter as Willow had ambushed their father as he pulled a child-sized sleigh up the packed-down snow of the drive.

Years later, there was snow and a sleigh, Allison and Willow, but the laughter was missing. In the silence, Allison felt sad and heavy.

She glanced at Willow and pictured the first time she'd seen her, tiny and screaming, her face purple and her gummy mouth open in that mewling wail only a newborn can make. Her dad gently had placed her new sister into her arms, and Allison had felt the warm weight of the new, little life settle against her. She had practiced holding babies with her stash of stuffed animals, but this was entirely different.

The baby's wailing softened like an ambulance racing off into the distance and her little sister had opened her eyes, a blue so deep they were almost purple. Allison smiled at her then and introduced herself.

"I'm Allison and I'm 10 years old, and I'm going to protect you," she had whispered to the infant. She had felt their dad's eyes on her as she said it, but Allison didn't care. She had needed the baby to know—right away—that her big sister would be there for her. She had thought of Alex as she said it, and the way that she hadn't been able to protect him.

The thoughts of her twin brother that day had made her picture something else: a day not of introductions, but good-byes. She had been 8 the day she had stood between her parents as they laid her brother to rest. Allison hadn't been able to look at his casket. She hadn't been able to picture Alex, with his bright brown eyes and freckles, lying quietly against the white satin pillow surrounded by his beloved hockey stick and collection of rocks. Alex had never been still or particularly obedient, and the thought of him lying so nicely confused her.

Her parents had argued about allowing Allison to attend her brother's funeral. She wouldn't understand, her mother had yelled, her ragged, defeated voice carrying through the walls of her parents' bedroom. But on the day of the funeral, Allison had put on her best outfit—the yellow sundress with the pretty flowers and matching shoes—and brushed her hair carefully, trying to make it cover the bandages that covered one side of her face. She didn't yet have a word for what she was feeling, trying to cover the gauze and tape, but it felt somehow wrong that a cut—just a stupid cut—was all that had happened to her when the same accident had killed her brother.

Allison had sat in the front row with her parents during the service, her dad absentmindedly patting her shoulder. She hadn't cried, because Alex just didn't look like Alex. He never made a face like the one the boy in the casket was making.

But as they lowered it into the ground, Allison felt her throat go tight and her stomach clench like it did when she had eaten too many hot dogs at the baseball game she'd attended one time with Alex and their grandparents. They were covering her brother with dirt. He'd had a knack for finding mud and dirt, but he'd always come clean. And suddenly, Allison realized he'd never come clean again.

She had looked up then, squinting in the too-bright sunshine. It didn't seem right to be burying Alex on such a pretty day, with fluffy, cotton-ball clouds puffing across the jewel-bright sky and the soft grass a carpet of green under her feet. Allison looked up and saw a willow tree, its wispy limbs bowed toward the ground and swaying in the breeze. The slender branches formed a dome, the type of secret hiding spot Alex would have loved. He would have charged through the waving branches and declared the shady, protected room his kingdom, the trunk his castle, and the limbs his castle walls. Allison pictured him living forever within the branches of the willow, happy and alive.

When she stared at the face of her new baby sister just two years later, she pictured that willow tree.

"Willow," she whispered to the newborn. "That's what we'll call you."

She had never told anyone, not even her parents, that she imagined Alex living in that willow tree. Her dad frowned as she looked up.

"Willow? Like the tree?"

Allison had nodded and snuggled her sister. Her dad glanced at her mom, who was propped up against pillows in the narrow bed, the paper-thin hospital gown hanging loosely against the ashen pallor of her neck. But her mom didn't smile or even look at her. Her eyes were staring at the far wall, like she saw something there no one else could.

"What do you think, sweetie?" Allison's dad had asked, his voice gentle as he looked at his wife.

Allison's mom slid her eyes from the wall, but she didn't seem to really see her husband. "I wanted an A name."

"No," Allison said, louder and sharper than she'd meant. "A" names were for her and Alex. She ran a finger down the thick, tough scar as she said it, a physical reminder of her brother.

Her dad had smiled at her then, the same bright, indulgent smile he gave her when she came bounding down the stairs to show him her spelling test or when she pulled him by the hand to sit and listen to her latest story.

"It's a beautiful name, Allison." He took his youngest daughter from Allison's hands and nuzzled her forehead. "Right, Willow?"

The snort of the reindeer pulled Allison back to the cold of Sweden. She wiped quickly at her wet eyes and tried to sniff quietly. She hadn't thought of that day in more than 14 years. Even Alex had faded to become just a memory of a boy she'd once played with and fought and loved with all her heart.

But the memory had tugged at something else. Willow's quiet, angry voice earlier hadn't been laced with hatred, but with sadness. She had heard that same defeated sadness in her mom's voice that day in the hospital, and she heard it weaving through Willow's, turning her words of defiance into mourning.

"Will," Allison said, and she coughed quickly when her voice hitched in her throat. "I'm happy you're here."

Willow turned to her then, finally looking into Allison's eyes for the first time since she'd arrived in Sweden. Her little sister held her stare for a moment then broke away, rolling her brown eyes—eyes that matched Alex's— and laughing harshly.

"You're happy I'm here? Good for you. Glad I could drag my ass half way across the world to make you *happy*," she said, her voice derisive.

Allison started. "Will, what did I—"

"Oh my god," Willow snapped. "Listen to you!" Her voice was getting louder, and the reindeer slowed, stamping in agitation. "What did you do? Are you seriously asking me that?"

Allison tried to lay a gloved hand on Willow's arm, but the girl roughly pulled away, pushing herself as far into the corner of the sleigh as she could.

"You left! You left Mom and Dad and ... and me. And you just," she sputtered, pointing hard, "you just don't care about anybody but yourself." Willow leapt to her feet, shoving the heavy blanket from her legs and making the whole sleigh jerk. The reindeer snorted and stamped, but Willow didn't look at them—she only glared at her sister.

Before Allison could stop her, Willow jumped from the sleigh, sinking into the powder up to her knees, and struggled through the deep drifts that lined the trail. Allison didn't think, she just jumped after her, straining her legs to move through the pile. Even through the layers, the cold of the deep snow seeped into her, biting, but Allison ignored it and pumped her legs harder, willing them to slide through.

"Will! Wait!"

But Willow didn't slow down, didn't even turn as she thrashed through the snow.

"Willow!" Allison shouted, her voice raw as she yelled. "Damn it, Willow, stop it!"

And with a screech of frustration, Willow stopped, slumped against the rough bark of a pine tree. It seemed to take ages for Allison to finally reach her, and when she did, she saw that her sister's face was wet with tears.

"You left," Willow whispered, her voice thick. "You left me all alone with her."

"I know, I'm sorry," Allison said, trying to pull Willow to her, but the younger girl pushed her away and leaned heavily against the tree.

"You *don't* know, Allie," she said, tears spilling over her eyelashes and streaming down her face. "She's just so *angry* all the time ... and I think I'm getting angry like her. I just ... it's like I'm never happy and I have no one to help."

Allison pulled in a sharp breath, the cold air burning. She had no idea. Her mom had always favored Willow; she thought it'd make things better if she left. She never knew ...

"She ... she hasn't treated you like she did me—"

Willow shook her head, and Allison sighed deeply, relieved her sister had at least been spared that.

"She says really awful things about you, Allie," Willow whispered. It made her voice sound very small, like she was no longer a 14-year-old girl, but that 5-year-old who woke up crying each night for weeks, afraid her mom had left like her dad. "I tried to tell Dad, but he just told me to ignore it ... and it's not like I can talk bad about Mom with *her* around ... his new, stupid, perfect family."

Willow scrubbed her face with her mittens, smearing the smudge of eyeliner Allison had noticed she'd started using at the outside edges of her eyes. "I'm just ... I don't know how to make Mom happy," Willow said, her voice shrill. "And she never says anything nice about you. I hate that you two don't get along."

That vacant stare that had made her mother's eyes seem haunted in the hospital after Willow was born had followed her home. Over the months, that look had turned hard, and it had turned on Allison.

There were moments of happiness, where the mom Allison had known before seemed to break down the hard barrier she'd erected and shine down on her oldest daughter. Allison had lived for these little bits of warm sunshine, but then the dark would return, and Allison would be left adrift in the storm.

Her mom had said terrible things to Allison during those storms. She had said she wished Allison had been killed in the crash and not Alex. She had said Allison was the reason her dad left.

Allison would retreat into her own head when her mother raged, ignoring the taunts and screams as best she could, and biting the inside of her cheek until she tasted blood to make sure her mom wouldn't see her eyes bright with tears.

Her mom had spared Willow, and sometimes Allison felt a horrible ache in her chest to see her mom share a joke with Willow or lovingly play with her hair, but mostly, she was thankful. Allison had made a promise to her little sister when she was born to protect her, and she intended to honor it.

But staring at the girl crying in the snow in front of her, Allison felt a sharp stab of pain in her chest. She hadn't honored that promise. She had left Willow alone with a broken woman and told herself it was for the best, that she was making things better by leaving.

It had been her dad who had convinced her to go two years before. She had been home on spring break, her senior year of college, and had just learned she'd been accepted to the prestigious anthropology internship in Sweden. Her mom's voice was barely audible as she glared at her oldest daughter and told her to never come back.

Allison had fled to her dad's condo across town and cried until the heaving in her chest made her dizzy. Her dad had reached across the dining room table then and covered her hand. "We remind her too much of him," he had said, his voice low and measured. "We'll never be more than a reminder of something horrible that happened to her."

Allison had nodded and squeezed her eyes shut. She didn't want to be a horrible reminder; she just wanted to be a daughter.

"Allie," Willow whispered, shaking Allison from the painful thoughts of her mom and the last time she'd spoken to her. "Do you know I didn't even know how Alex died?" She smiled sadly and ran her mittened hand down the faded pink scar along Allison's cheek.

"Do you know what that's like," Willow continued, her voice soft. "I grew up in a house full of photos of a boy I never met. I heard nothing but stories of how perfect he was and always felt I could never be as wonderful as him."

"Willow," Allison interrupted, "that's not true. Mom and Dad love you."

Willow waved her away. "I know that, I do, but do you have any idea what it's like to grow up with a ghost you never knew? I thought ... I thought if I could just be like you, it'd be like Mom had Alex back. You were his twin; I thought I could be your twin, too. And then you left and ... I didn't know he'd died in a car crash until someone told me at school. They said Mom had been drunk and crashed and killed her own son."

Allison gasped. "That's not ... Will, Mom wasn't drinking, it was the other driver. Have you thought that all this time?"

Willow shrugged. "Who else was going to tell me different? Mom wouldn't talk about it."

Tears pricked Allison's eyes. She pulled her sister into a hug and felt the tears gather against her lashes when Willow didn't pull away.

"I'm so sorry I left," she whispered, her voice muffled against the knit hat pulled down low over her sister's head. "I wasn't a sister to you, but I promise I'll make it up to you. I'll protect you."

And as she said it, she knew it was true. Her sister needed her, and if that meant leaving Sweden, she'd do it without blinking. Her arm around Willow, Allison led them back through the track they'd pushed through the deep snow to the waiting sleigh.

"You know," she said quietly, shaking out the heavy blanket and draping it back over their cold legs, "I may have sucked at the whole sister thing for the past two years, but that didn't mean I stopped keeping tabs on you."

Willow looked at her and frowned, but her brown eyes were warm now, curious, and the tears that streaked down her face had dried.

"Dad's been giving me a play-by-play of your Quiz Bowl meets," Allison said. "He even sent me a recording of the one that ran on TV last month." And Allison was happy to see her sister's blonde eyebrows shoot up, disappearing under her hat. She nudged her sister with her shoulder, then turned away, staring at the reindeer's bristle of thick, gray fur and the slender leather reins that attached her to them. "That guy next to you was pretty cute."

Beside her, Willow groaned in embarrassment, but a quick glance showed that her cheeks, already red with cold, flushed a deeper crimson.

"You mean Mike. He's annoying and a year older than me." Willow was silent for a moment, sniffling back the last of the tears, and Allison wasn't sure if the younger girl was hoping she would ask more, but the moment passed. "Anyway, what about you? When do I get to meet George? Dad said he had a funny accent."

Allison pursed her lips. "Dad would say that. And the accent's not funny, it's Scottish." She paused, thinking of George, with his easy smile and green eyes. It felt a bit strange to think she'd had a boyfriend for almost two years whom her mom knew nothing about. Something twisted in

Allison's stomach to think about it—leaving Sweden to go back home would probably mean leaving George, right when they'd started making plans for the future. She wondered if he'd come with her, but told herself it wouldn't matter either way.

The sisters fell back into silence, but it wasn't the heavy kind. The reindeer pulled them through the pine forest, the world a silvery glow of snow below and stars above. Allison loved the quiet of a snowy wood—it made everything soft, almost muted.

It was the type of place she could imagine fantasy coming to life. Just at the edges of vision, laughing just outside the range of hearing, Allison imagined fairies and trolls, gnomes and spirits. In the snow and ice, they seemed to follow her, dancing and singing just out of sight. She found herself sometimes peering out the corner of her eye or turning her head sharply, always almost certain she'd catch a vision of her dreams.

In the snug seat of the sleigh, Willow burrowed deeper into the heavy blanket and leaned her head against Allison's shoulder.

"You'll really come home, Allie?" she asked quietly, a whisper of a thought.

Allison thought of George again—of him touching her scar lightly the first night he'd stayed over and asking what had happened, to just a few days before when he'd offered to ride ahead to get the cabin ready for her and Willow. She took a deep breath, the frigid air burning her lungs and sharpening her senses. It felt good.

"Yes, Will, I'll really come home. You can live with me if you want, or I can try to make things better with Mom. Whatever you need."

"Thank you," the younger girl whispered. "Tell me a story like you used to," Willow said after a moment, her breath puffing out in a white cloud. She pulled the blanket up closer to her chin and tucked her feet under her.

Allison slid her eyes to Willow and raised one eyebrow. Her little sister hadn't asked for a story in years.

"There once was a girl named Will," she said, her voice rising and falling with the cadence of a poem, "whose pale skin made her look really ill."

Beside her, Willow sat up and grimaced, pulling the blanket away from Allison. "You suck at rhyming," she giggled, the first laugh Allison had heard from her in two years. It made happiness fizz in her chest. "And I'm pale? You practically blend in with the snow. Besides, I believe this is called 'alabaster,' not pale."

"Looks like someone finally watched those 'Anne of Green Gables' DVDs I gave you years ago."

"Allie, the only thing worse than those movies is your skill at rhyming."

Allison gasped in mock horror. "Anne graced you with a middle name, so have some respect, young lady."

Willow crooked one eyebrow and let her Cupid mouth drop open a bit, looking incredibly like a 14-year-old. "More like middle lame."

Allison shook her head, but she was laughing easily. She'd missed Willow, but even more than that, she realized she missed seeing her grow up. The girl next to her was no longer a child, she was becoming a woman who was wearing makeup and had crushes and was trying to figure everything out on her own. Allison felt a hollow sadness at the thought of everything she'd missed, but she felt something else, too: a bubble of hope. She'd help her sister grow up; she'd maybe even make things right with her mom.

"Really, Allie, tell me a story."

Allison looked up at the sky, thinking. Across the sky, a finger of pearlescent green hooked across the darkness, illuminating the tops of the pines for a moment before darting back to the horizon. Ahead, the track through the close trees thinned, and Allison could just see the vast, white plain of the winter-covered lake.

A story. Willow had been five that evening when they'd followed their grandparents through the twilight forest and into the clearing, the tall grass rustling in the breeze. Her dad had left just days before, and her mom had dropped the girls at their grandparents' house and driven off, sending a shower of rocks spraying into the air. Allison had watched the lonely dirt road until even the plume of dust from her mother's car had vanished, then she'd turned around and put a smile on her face for her little sister.

On that walk a week later, Allison and Willow had followed their grandfather to the edge of the clearing. He had clicked off the flashlight, and the evening suddenly flickered a brilliant, lustrous gold. Beside her, Willow had gasped and pulled Allison by the hand into the field of dancing fireflies. The thin, green grass brushed against her little sister's round belly, but Willow didn't seem to mind as she peered closely at the glowing bugs, giggling madly as they flew around her, their tiny bodies pulsing like miniature suns in the night.

"Allie," Willow had breathed, her voice quiet with awe, "who are they?"

It was the way she'd worded it—who, not what—that made Allison tell her the story as they stood in the field surrounded by fireflies. With her eyes on the dancing lights making tentative swoops across the sky from the horizon, it was the story she told again.

"When the world was young, fairies and sprites and goblins walked the earth," Allison said, her voice quiet in the stillness. She imagined those creatures of fantasy scurrying behind the sleigh, straining their little ears to hear her tale.

"And in this world before the stars or the moon, there were two sisters, Sister Day and Sister Night," Willow picked up, her voice clear as a bell as she recounted the tale Allison had told her countless times growing up.

"But Sister Night, the younger child, was afraid of the darkness and the strange creatures that came out to play. She begged Mother Earth to give her light in the dark, but Mother Earth had nothing to give," Allison said, her eyes closed as her story played out in her mind. She fell into its cadence like a warm bath, remembering the rise and fall of her grandpa's voice as he told similar tales around the late-night campfires during summers at the cabin in northern Michigan.

"Sister Day loved her sister more than anything else in the new world — more than the fairies that played in the fields of flowers or the sprites that sang in the ocean. She was older, stronger and bigger than the little night child, so she traveled to Mother Earth with an idea. She would give some of herself to the night, making a light in the darkness to take away the fright of her sister. And Mother Earth, so moved by the love between the two sisters, agreed.

"Sister Day breathed brightness into the night. She became the stars and the fireflies and the northern lights.

And Sister Night was no longer afraid and saw that the strange creatures of the night were beautiful and kind. But best of all, the two sisters were finally able to explore the new world together."

Allison sighed the tiniest bit as she finished, and she heard Willow do the same beside her.

The reindeer pawed the ground a bit as they left the cover of trees, their hoofs crunching in the packed snow. The frozen lake spread before them like a white plain, snow-covered mountains ahead and the forest behind.

Just beyond the ice, Allison spied the tendril of smoke drifting from the log cabin George had gone ahead to prepare. Inside, there was a fire and hot tea, a warm barn for the reindeer and soft beds for her and Willow. Her lungs aching from the cold and her cheeks numb, she threw her head back, a bubbling laugh escaping her throat as she gazed above.

The velvet blue sky stretched from horizon to horizon and the glittering wash of stars seemed close enough to reach out and grab. And across it all, the dancing flame of the Northern Lights undulated on an unseen current. Greens and purples and pinks and colors for which there were no words. They swirled and darted and waved to an unheard chorus that Allison was sure was singing just on the edges of hearing. If she closed her eyes and let the colors and shapes flit across her eyelids, she could almost hear it. It was the sound of sisters laughing and comforting each other. Allison knew then that she would do everything she could to be the light for Willow's world.

Beside her, Willow gasped and matched Allison's bubbling laugh.

"Magic," Willow whispered.

And for the first time in years, Allison believed.

No Place Like Home

By Dani Stone

Stacie checked her BlackBerry for new messages as she waited for her friend to arrive.

Nothing.

Audrey was only a few minutes late, but Stacie anxiously scanned the parking lot for her friend's car. She had news, big news, news that kept her up so late the night before she found herself watching Chuck Norris' Total Gym infomercial. She not only watched the entire 30-minute program, she was actually looking for a pen to write down the telephone number when she heard Brian's voicemail message replay in her mind: "Stacie, it's me, um, Brian. I miss you. We need to talk."

She stopped looking for a pen and decided she would not be making any big decisions until she heard what Brian had to say, even if it meant missing out on all the Chuck Norris bad-assery.

Audrey was now ten minutes late. Stacie noticed the restaurant was filling up early with Christmas shoppers funneling in from the strip mall across the street. It was the first week of November and stores that hadn't already jumped the gun the previous month by putting the Elf on a Shelf next to a Jack o' Lantern were in full-on festive mode.

Stacie was glad she'd talked the manager in to letting her sit on the patio. The weather hadn't turned bone-chilling yet, and she knew once she told Audrey about the message, they would need time to dissect it. She was also trying to avoid another "ugly animal vest" incident. On a previous visit, an impatient customer wearing a dingy gray faux fur vest that looked like it had mange or was in serious need of grooming approached their table and angrily read them the riot act about chatting too long while other hungry diners waited in line.

Stacie and Audrey, embarrassed by Ms. Ugly Animal Vest's audacity and fearing what someone who would wear that in public would do if she were denied a spring roll much longer, had left to continue their conversation elsewhere.

When she finally saw Audrey walking quickly through the patio gate, Stacie rose for a hug. Audrey was tiny, "five-foot nothing," her Grandma Jordan would say. Stacie smiled when she thought of this phrase. It was one of the many Grandma Jordanisms she remembered from her childhood. Suddenly, an image of her grandmother's cozy kitchen flashed in her mind, the kitchen that literally vanished in an instant during that horrible spring day. She was pulled back to reality by Audrey's animated rant.

Quickly unwrapping the scarf from her neck, Audrey huffed, "I swear to the baby Jesus in his snuggly winter coat, what is wrong with these people? They stop to gawk at Christmas lights and end up driving 20 miles per hour. We haven't even carved a turkey yet. Step. It. Up." Audrey enunciated those last few words, tapping her foot in time. Stacie was used to her friend showing up late with an entertaining story, but now it was her turn.

After they'd both ordered steaming cups of hot chai to kill the chill, Audrey broke the silence.

"Okay, so spill it. Why does your face look like that?"

"Like what?"

"I know when something's up," Audrey replied.

Stacie took a deep breath and quietly muttered, "Brian called."

When it registered, Audrey's eyes became little cartoon saucers. "Brian? Selfish Brian? Always looked good in a suit Brian? Broke your heart Brian?"

Stacie cut her off before Audrey could bring back more painful memories.

"Yes! All those Brians. He called my house yesterday and left a message."

Like a cat, Audrey's eyes quickly changed from half-dollars of surprise to slits of suspicion. "Annnnd?"

Stacie cleared her throat and with an even tone repeated Brian's 12-word message: "Stacie, it's me, um, Brian. I miss you. We need to talk."

Audrey waited. "That's it?"

Stacie nodded as a brisk Kansas wind kicked up. She flipped the collar on her black wool coat and continued, "I haven't called back. Every time I try, my fingers tremble and my throat closes up, and at this point, I just can't imagine what there is to say." She took a sip of her chai and added, "Did you catch the part about him missing me?"

Audrey slapped the metal table with her hand so hard, her rings made a loud "clink" sound that would've startled other patrons who were brave enough to be outside with them. "He misses you? Well, hell yes! He should. You're fantastic and he's ... he's ... Brian the Bonehead."

Stacie giggled and just as quickly, the furrowed brow was back.

A young waiter appeared, looking cold and annoyed to be outside. With her stomach in knots earlier, Stacie had already declined a menu, so the acne-faced ambassador turned his attention to Audrey and asked, "Ma'am, are you gonna eat?"

Stacie cringed. Audrey was ten years older and her 40th birthday was rapidly approaching. Lately, she'd become a little touchy about it.

Audrey flashed the man-child her sweetest cougar smile and replied, "I'll tell you what: You don't *ever* call me 'ma'am' again, you keep these cups full of hot chai, you let us chat and we'll make sure you get a good tip. Okay?"

The waiter shrugged, mumbled and walked back inside as Stacie thought, "We will never see him again and this tea is going to get very cold."

Audrey dove right in to the interrogation. "Sooo, why do you think he called? What does he want? Are you going to call him back? Can I be on the extension when you do? "

As she watched Audrey lean farther across the table with each question, her wide eyes and dark curls giving her a momentary Medusa appearance, Stacie began to wonder if it was really a good idea to tell her about the phone call. Audrey was a good friend, but very protective, and now, sure enough, here she was, ready to nip at Brian's ankles like an angry little Pomeranian.

"I don't know. I don't know and no, you can absolutely not be on the extension," Stacie admonished.

Shrugging her shoulders under her leopard coat, Audrey said, "I can't believe you didn't call him immediately. I mean, this is wild. It's been, what, two years?"

Stacie stared across the parking lot at the Bed Bath & Beyond in the strip mall. A festive, obviously industrious employee had festooned the "O" in the sign with an oversized Christmas wreath that completely covered the "N" and the "D" making it look like Bed Bath and Be-Yo!

It had not only been two years, it had been two years and five months, to be exact, since the last time she saw Brian in person. She was still mourning the recent death of her grandmother when Audrey had surprised her with plane tickets for a girls' weekend to Las Vegas. "Because who can be sad when you're taking inappropriate pictures with a fake George Clooney at Madame Tussauds Wax Museum?" she'd explained.

When Brian drove her to the airport that morning to join Audrey, they were both hiding red-rimmed eyes under their sunglasses. The night before, as she packed swimsuits and sundresses into her suitcase, he told her he had accepted a position with a pharmaceutical company in Phoenix. He explained he hadn't consulted her because the job was, "too good to pass up" and he "assumed she would be happy wherever *he* was."

When she had asked him if he ever thought about marriage, his reply was the same as always: "Baby, I love you, but right now I have to be married to my job. Please be patient." After years of hearing the same selfish spiel, she decided she'd been patient enough. He moved to Phoenix three weeks later, alone.

The women had planned to spend that weekend sunning on the manmade beach at Mandalay Bay, playing nickel slots and checking out the view from the VooDoo Lounge at Rio. Instead, Stacie found herself mourning her grandmother *and* her relationship, spending much of the trip in her complimentary hotel robe, ordering silver room-service trays full of carbohydrates while Audrey cooed, "Are you sure you don't wanna get out tonight, sweetie? I hear the Blue Man Group is fun."

As Stacie predicted, the waiter never came back, and when the cold air began to numb their fingers and toes, the women decided to go their separate ways for the evening. The conversation wasn't helping Stacie much, anyway. She was glad she told Audrey, because now the words were out there in the universe and she knew it wasn't a dream. Audrey listened intently like a good friend, but her comments consisted primarily of, "Do you think he's contracted a heinous STD and now his doctor is making him call his former lovers?" and "Should I have my brother Jason use his Scarface voice and tell him not to call anymore?"

Stacie declined the thoughtful Scarface offer, thanked her for her concern, and promised she would call when she figured out what to do next.

When Stacie got home that night, she didn't take off her shoes on the rug by the door, hang her keys on the "do-daddy" (another Grandma Jordanism) or put her purse on the counter next to the kitschy coffee cup rack as she usually did. Instead, she walked straight through the kitchen and in to the living room to look at the answering machine.

The light blinked and a red number "1" indicated she had a new message waiting. It had been approximately 27 hours since Brian left her the 12-word message of hope, frustration, curiosity? She still didn't know how she felt about it.

As she pushed the play button, she closed her eyes and thought, "Please don't let the message begin with, 'I visited my doctor the other day and he said I should call you.'" The automated voice announced the time and date of the message. Stacie let out the breath she didn't realize she'd been holding when she heard Audrey's voice. "Hey Stacie, it's me, sorry I wasn't much help tonight. Truth is, I got nothin'. The you-and-Brian thing always seemed bigger than both of you at the time. You know you won't let this go until you call him, so, call him. Okay, that's it. See you, love you, bye."

Feeling a little dejected there wasn't another message but not quite ready to return Brian's call, she walked to the kitchen where she took off her shoes by the rug, hung her keys on the do-daddy and placed her purse on the counter next to the kitschy coffee cup rack.

One hour after cueing up her Celtic Woman CD and turning the volume high, Stacie had Riverdanced her way around the house, folding laundry, doing dishes and tidying up. During the day, she might leave a few dishes on the counter or gym clothes balled up on the floor, but by the time she went to bed, she wanted everything in its place. She often wondered if she got her clean gene from her grandmother. Grandma Jordan had poor eyesight, almost legally blind, but her house was always spotless. Not even dust bunnies could outrun her.

Stacie dried the last coffee cup and hung it on the rack. It read, "Grind Here Often," a gift from her mother, "to add to your crazy collection," she'd said with a wave of her hand. Stacie doubted her mother knew the phrase was a double entendre. Once when Stacie's parents had come over for coffee after antique shopping, Stacie's father (who *was* quite aware of the double naughty meaning) handed his wife the cup and shouted loud enough for Stacie to hear in the next room, "Hey, Honey, grind here often?"

Without missing a beat, Stacie shouted back, "Not in my kitchen you don't! I cook food in there for heaven's sake!" Her father belted out his familiar deep gravelly laugh, created by years of inhaling Marlboro 100s. Stacie's mother just smiled and said, "You two are a mess."

Before heading to bed, Stacie decided to unwind by watching the handsome Anderson Cooper on CNN. Anderson was much too handsome to be a roving reporter. For a man who covered wars, natural disasters and religious uprisings, he maintained a surprisingly pampered appearance.

After flopping down and turning on the television, Stacie smoothed her grandmother's blanket folded neatly on the back of the couch. The blanket still had bits of caked mud on the edges from being thrown into the dirt by the storm, but she couldn't bear to wash it, not when it still held the scent of her grandmother, who always smelled like Noxzema face wash.

After a few minutes of watching Anderson and his angel-kissed blue eyes, Stacie's gaze shifted to a small table beside the television that held her favorite picture in the house, the sleigh ride. She'd looked at the photo hundreds of times growing up, but since her grandmother's death, it had found a new home, *her* home.

Stacie recalled how excited Grandma Jordan became whenever she talked about the night of the sleigh ride, how her husband had surprised her with it when they were dating. Stacie never had the opportunity to meet her grandfather, Allen. He died of cancer a few years before she was born. Her grandmother called it "one of life's cruelest things."

The photograph was black-and-white, but after hearing the story so many times, she could see the colors in her mind. The red sleigh the two sleek, brown horses with snow falling on their manes and bridles; the thick, grey wool blanket covering her grandmother's legs, one gloved hand holding on to her felt hat, the other holding her grandfather's hand. The picture was more than just two teenagers going for a ride in the snow; her grandfather proposed in the sleigh that night. The picture symbolized a beginning: two young lovers riding into the future, excited for what they would make together—two sons, a daughter, a thriving antique business—blissfully unaware of the heartache, and the cancer and the storm. When volunteers discovered the frame in the ruins, they were shocked to find the glass still intact. The little picture in the gunmetal frame bordered by delicate, etched filigree had survived the tornado.

The next morning, Stacie made her way to the coffee pot where the green light signaled her favorite beverage was done brewing and waiting for her. She adored everything about coffee: the way it smelled, the way it tasted, the way a warm cup felt in her hand when she held it and the way the caffeine helped emerge her from what the young pharmacy techs at work called "the cocoon of the beast."

Sipping her coffee and feeling the beast slowly retreating, Stacie finally noticed the writing on the cup she had absent-mindedly plucked off the rack that morning: "Put your big girl panties on and deal with it." Looking at her phone, she decided that's exactly what she would do.

Stacie flicked through the caller ID until she found the telephone number Brian called from. She wasn't surprised when she realized it was the same cell phone number he had when they were dating. As a pharmaceutical sales rep, he was always cramming his brain with new drug names, side effects and dosing instructions. He used to say it was comforting to have things in his life he had committed to memory so long ago that he couldn't forget them, like his parents' telephone number, his padlock for the gym in junior high and his favorite password, "penicillin."

As she dialed the number, her finger pushed each button firmly for emphasis. By the time she got to the final digit, her hands were shaking and she cleared her throat in a loud, exaggerated fashion. She didn't want their first conversation in more than two years to begin with her sounding like Peter in the "Brady Bunch" episode where puberty causes his voice to become a series of croaks and shrieks during a live performance of "Time to Change."

On the first ring, Brian picked up, but she could barely hear him say "hello" through the cacophony of other voices in the background.

"Brian, this is Stacie, can you hear me?"

"Yes, yes I can!" Brian shouted. Stacie heard "Jock Jams" music start up in the background and wondered if she'd caught him sitting courtside at a basketball game. "Stacie, listen, I'm in Los Angeles! I'm going in to a kickoff meeting for a new drug! They're just starting! Can I call you back? Two hours tops! Will you be there?"

Unless she wanted to talk to Brian with a loud bass thumping in the background, she'd have to say, "yes," even though truthfully, she was a little disappointed.

"Sure, okay," she muttered.

Before they were disconnected, Stacie thought she heard him say, "Awesome!" but she didn't know if he was talking about their upcoming conversation or the launch party that awaited him.

She was sitting in perfect posture on the edge of her bed, as if she were waiting for the captain to announce, "We're getting ready for descent, so please make sure your seats and tray tables are in the full and upright position." After the call, her body felt very heavy, so she slumped back against the pillow, pouting. She'd run through several scenarios in her mind about this phone call, but getting blown off for a raucous, new Rx celebration was not one of them.

After two years without him, she had finally gotten to the point where she stopped wondering what he was doing every day, stopped wondering who he was with, stopped dreaming about him. Within the past year, she had even packed away all the pictures taken of them as a couple that had plastered the corkboard in her shared office at the pharmacy, or had stood in frames perched on tables and bookshelves around her spacious apartment. The pain of his leaving had been more than she could bear at first, but eventually, she just felt numb.

It was Audrey who convinced her to put the snapshots away, saying, "How can you bring a new man home when Brian is going to be staring them down from the mountains and the Tree of Life?" She referred, of course, to photos taken while hiking in Colorado and a business trip-turned- getaway to Disney World's Animal Kingdom in Orlando.

Unfortunately, there had been very few "new men" to bring home. She'd dated approximately three men in that time, but none had come close to making her feel the way Brian had.

Audrey told her she was sabotaging herself and even asked if she could write to Dr. Phil on Stacie's behalf to see if she could be a guest on the show. "He can be a hard ass, but he really gets through to people," her friend declared one morning after they met for breakfast to discuss a particularly bad dating experience. That one ended with Stacie making an excuse about being sick so she could avoid inviting her suitor inside her apartment at the end of the night after he'd hinted about sleeping over, slyly adding that he, "made the best omelets in town." Stacie had retorted, "Maybe, but so does the chef at IHOP, and he doesn't require I get naked first."

Taking a deep breath, she opened the drawer to her nightstand and reached in, shuffling past emery boards, a half-read book about the grieving process, assorted lip balms and eye drops until she found what she was looking for: a strip of photos from a coin-operated booth taken over six years ago on her first date with Brian at the fair. She studied all five pictures. Already so comfortable with each other after spending so much time together in a study group in college, Brian had his arm wrapped around her, their cheeks pressed together side by side. With their tan skin and matching blonde hair, they looked like an ad for suntan oil when they smiled or those super-happy people you see on brochures for Hawaii.

Their first kiss was documented on the strip. After smiling and making silly faces in the first four photos, as the light flashed for the last photo, Brian said, "Look at me," and kissed her on the lips. That kiss led to another until a knock on the photo booth reminded them there were waiting people outside.

Later, she'd told her college roommate, "That man has a kiss that could break hearts. I just hope it won't be mine." And though the kissing was always good, as well as other things, their independent natures and only-child personas were often a source of contention. They were both pursuing master's degrees in tough, competitive fields, and neither one seemed to know how to give. If they were children on a playground, they'd both want to rule the sandbox.

"We're too much alike," she thought. "That's why things didn't work out. We're both too selfish. Now, he's somewhere in Los Angeles and *still* putting work first."

The night before she left for Las Vegas, she had told him she loved him but couldn't leave her family and rearrange her own career goals, just because he expected her to. That if he went to Phoenix, they were through. She called his bluff and lost.

The memory made her bolt upright on the bed. She opened the nightstand drawer and shoved the picture inside, closing it so hard she made the bedside lamp teeter, nearly knocking it to the floor.

By December 15, Stacie's pharmacy had been playing Christmas carols for a solid month. Her store received the standard-issue holiday music CD, played in an endless loop.

As she filled prescriptions for cough syrup with codeine, and other common winter-flu medications, she listened to Mariah Carey belt out "All I Want for Christmas Is You" in her characteristic falsetto. She often wondered if Mariah had dogs, and if those dogs growled painfully when she hit the near-impossible G7 octave. It had been approximately two weeks since Brian's last message. She had to give it to the guy for persistence.

He'd been calling for weeks! He obviously didn't have her new cell phone number and for that, she was grateful. The messages ranged from light-hearted banter, ("Hey, Stace, come on, return my call, all the cool kids are doing it,") to slightly desperate, ("Stacie, I got your email and I swear if you'll just pick up, we can talk this out"). She'd written the email one week after returning his initial call:

Brian,

I know this seems impersonal but please don't call anymore. There is nothing left of us and nothing left to discuss. We've both built different lives and we need to continue doing what we've been doing for over two years, moving on.

Stacie

After she had sent it and emptied the last of her Bitch brand wine in to a coffee cup with "Hey Cutie, Can I Have a Refill?" written on it, Stacie wiped away a tear and raised a glass to the television, where she'd been watching a *Sex and the City* marathon. Miranda would be proud of her. Charlotte would scold her for drinking wine alone out of a coffee cup, but she didn't care. She hadn't been in the mood for dainty sipping; she wanted to guzzle.

Looking out the tiny drive-thru window of the pharmacy, Stacie noticed snowflakes beginning to fall, adding another layer to the two inches that had fallen the night before. Watching the snow glisten as it floated past the lamps in the parking lot, she began to wish she hadn't agreed to trade with the usual night-shift pharmacist.

She loved watching snowfall, preferably when she was sitting snuggly in the oversized bay window of her apartment. The night pharmacist, Ben, was a father of four, and when he showed her the picture of his first-grade daughter decked out in the reindeer costume she would be wearing for the school Christmas play, her heart melted. She couldn't say "no" to little Dasher and those brown antlers perched atop auburn ringlets, so she agreed to cover his shift.

She was at an age when she was starting to think about being a mother herself, but she was missing an important component: the daddy. She wasn't interested in pulling what she called a "starlet move," swooping in to an impoverished country and adopting a child. She didn't want to be a single mom. She wanted the whole package, a family.

She used to daydream about the towheaded babies she and Brian would have, all the camping trips they'd take and the Christmas Eves with everyone in matching pajamas, huddled on the couch for a reading of "'Twas The Night Before Christmas." Without Grandma Jordan's mashed potatoes and Brian's hip-swiveling, lip-curling rendition of Elvis' "Blue Christmas," the last few holidays had seemed empty; here she was, preparing to coast through another one.

When her shift ended at 8:00 p.m., Stacie buttoned her wool coat, wrapped her scarf around her head and her neck, pulled on her black Isotoners, and walked to the door to wait for Audrey. They'd planned to meet for coffee and Christmas shopping at a nearby bookstore.

With the snow falling and the stores decorated with wreaths and Garlands, it looked almost like a Thomas Kinkaide painting. Looking out the glass door, she watched for her friend. Ten minutes late. No surprise there. She should've known better than to bundle up before she saw Audrey pull into the parking lot. With the heat on in the pharmacy, she was actually starting to sweat. She thought about taking her gloves off when something caught her eye in the distance. Winding its way around the Hallmark store, led by two beautiful, sleek, black horses, was a red sleigh. She could see two drivers in front, one holding the reins, the other bundled in a down parka that looked more suited for mountain climbing on Everest than a casual ride through the snow. She couldn't see the passenger.

In the past, she'd seen a man offering sleigh rides around Christmas, but never this early and certainly not in a snowfall that looked far from letting up. As they got closer, she marveled at how the horses seemed to be stepping in unison and how majestic they looked, even with their ankles wrapped in what looked like festive red legwarmers. The driver turned the reins, and then with a firm grip, pulled back until the team stopped in front of the pharmacy. Stacie got her first look at the passenger, a small woman waving wildly in a matching leopard coat and hat.

"What are you doing?" Stacie laughed as she approached the sleigh.

The driver left his perch, and opened the door for her. His partner sat hunched with his hood pulled down.

Audrey hugged her friend and shrieked, "How much fun is *this*?"

Stacie had never ridden in a sleigh and she had to admit, though the snow was falling at a pretty good pace, she felt happier than she had in weeks. She laughed again and said, "You really know how to make an entrance, don't you, lady?"

Audrey smiled, shrugged and sat down, raising a corner of the checked, red-and-black blanket she'd been covering her legs with, inviting her friend to share. Stacie thanked the driver for his chivalrous help. His face was weathered and little icicles were starting to form on his moustache.

He smiled, nodded and returned to his post. When Stacie was tucked under her half of the blanket, he barked a command and with a flick of the reins, the horses began to trot again, effortlessly pulling the weight of the sleigh behind them.

As the horses took them gliding past the Big & Tall Men's Store and Bed Bath & Be-Yo, Audrey spoke quickly, sounding like an old cassette tape rewinding, "I know I said I supported your decision to cut ties with Brian, but you really shouldn't listen to me in matters of the heart. Remember, I broke up with the last guy I dated because he made of fun of my dog sweaters. I told him my little daschunds get cold in the winter, but he just rolled his eyes, so I told him to leave right in the middle of dinner and I ate his portion of pad thai." Audrey was on a roll. "You were in a rough place. He was fresh out of graduate school. Things are different now. You're both settled." Stacie held up her hand and surprisingly, Audrey stopped.

"No. I can't do it."

"But you didn't even talk to him. You never gave him a chance," Audrey reasoned.

Stacie tried to hold on to her sleigh-ride-high, but it was quickly wearing off.

The horses slowed to a crawl again and when they came to a complete stop, they were in front of the bookstore. Audrey slid out from under the blanket and picked up her purse. With a nervous smile, she said, "Soooo, Charlie—that's the driver—and I are going inside for a latte. I bet he's more of a black coffee fan, but I'm going to introduce him to the joy that is steamed milk, whipped cream and mocha. Don't be mad. The sleigh ride wasn't my idea."

The driver shook his head and opened Audrey's door, leaving Stacie sitting in confusion.

"You two are going? What am *I* supposed to do?"

For the first time since their short ride, the driver spoke. Pointing at the back of his silent partner, he said, "Ask him, sweetheart, 'cause he's payin' good money for this little song and dance."

From the driver's seat, Brian turned around and pushed the hood of his parka back so she could see his face. He smiled, waved and confidently said, "Hi, Stace."

Looking at the face she missed for all those years, she simultaneously wanted to jump up and hug him, but also wanted to beat her fists in to his chest, though he probably wouldn't feel it through that enormous coat. Instead, she maintained her composure and turned to glare at her betrayer.

Brian stepped in to the sleigh with her, Audrey and the driver already shuffling inside for coffee. He sat down so close, she could feel his breath and see how red his cheeks were from the cold. His face was as familiar as her own, and she still remembered every detail. From his hazel eyes to the scar above his right brow, acquired when he was 5 years old, courtesy of a coffee table, his face was like home. Her hands started to shake and she could feel her heart racing.

"Brian, this is so nice but—"

"Please, just listen. You have to let me say this. I know in your email you said we had to move on with our lives, and I tried. I really did. I even dated someone, it got serious and we planned to move in together."

Stacie looked down and felt tears sting her eyes while he continued.

"We started looking for apartments together but the closer the day came to move, the more I realized I couldn't do it."

Brian knelt down so he could see Stacie's face. "The only true happiness I've ever known was with you."

The snow mixed with the tears on her cheeks as Stacie looked at him and sobbed, "You. Left. Me. You expected me to follow and when I didn't, you went anyway. You can't undo that."

Sitting beside her again, it was his turn to choke back tears. "I thought the job offer in Phoenix would be good for both of us. When you didn't come with me, I was angry and hurt. I was so focused on my career and my financial future that everything else came second. I just didn't realize *you* were my everything else." He stood up and began to swipe at tears with the back of his hand. The heartbreak in his voice was palpable.

When Brian got to Phoenix, he continued to reach out to her, calling to say "goodnight" and sending a few letters, but they never could bridge the distance between them. She knew she had been depressed after her grandmother died, but had she been unreasonable and stubborn, too?

The weight of the last few years combined with his unexpected appearance and the sudden onset of emotion was too much to bear alone. She jumped up, sending her blanket to the floor and grabbed his cold cheeks in her hands. Their lips met immediately and he wrapped his arms around her waist. Between kisses and tears, they both gasped for air and traded, "I'm sorry's" until they were exhausted.

Still standing in the sleigh and locked in a hug, Stacie laid her head on his chest and looked at the horses waiting patiently for their next command. She suddenly understood why Brian hadn't shown up at the pharmacy and just walked through the door: He needed something *big*.

"You remembered," she whispered. The picture of her grandparents in the sleigh the night he'd proposed. He'd wanted to show her their love could be that special, *was* that special.

As they walked inside the bookstore to save Charlie from Audrey, Brian kissed her hand and whispered, "One more little surprise. I hope that's okay."

Approaching the table, Stacie could hear Audrey regaling Charlie with a recap of the latest "Real Housewives of New Jersey" episode. He looked surprisingly intrigued. It was then she noticed two cups of coffee awaiting their arrival. Brian picked up his recycled paper cup, the same one clutched by every other caffeine-seeker in the place. He smiled, nodded to the one next to his and said, "Another one for your collection."

Inside the red ceramic mug, a talented barista had created a perfect foam heart perched atop her favorite hazelnut latte. Happy tears filled her eyes as she gazed at the illustration of Dorothy's ruby red slippers underneath the phrase, "There's No Place Like Home."

The Escape

By Megan Barlog

It started with a lie. One of those small ones you don't really think twice about, because it seems like a good idea at the time. A lie that isn't supposed to hurt anybody.

I'd told many lies before that day, and I've told a few hundred since. It's a way of life here in the Dome. For guys like me, a lie can mean the difference between life and death. The large force field that encases our city like a snow globe may protect our city from the harsh realities of the outside world, but it cannot protect us from each other.

It was uncharacteristically warm for winter the day I told it. The weather managers at Dome Corp were feeling benevolent, I guess. As I polished Clyde, one of the Stable's animaltron horses (and my personal project), my mind was preoccupied with machine parts I needed to order, animaltrons I had to rewire, and what it would take to get out of this oversized snow globe of a city. I was imagining riding a giant rocket through the Dome's force field when the sound of quick steps entering the building distracted me. I turned and caught a glimpse of red hair before it disappeared into the adjacent stall. Stuffing the polishing rag into my pocket, I quietly walked over to the partition dividing my stall from the next.

A girl with long locks of wavy red hair sat crouched on the ground with her arms hugging her knees to her chest. Her hair cascaded around her, hiding her face as she rested her forehead on her knees. I could tell from her breathing she'd been running long before reaching the Stable.

I shifted my weight slightly and the old wooden floorboards creaked. The girl whipped her head up to look at me, her bangs clinging to her sweaty face. She froze, and her eyes grew wide. For a moment, we just stared at each other, her brown eyes boring into my silver ones.

Then I heard the men. They were outside the building, but their voices grew louder as they approached. The girl tensed—she must have heard them too. They entered the Stable shouting, but I couldn't tear my eyes away from her. I saw fear in her eyes, and some other emotion I couldn't put my finger on.

"Anyone in here?" asked one man.

In a hushed voice, another man told the others, "She ran in here, I'm sure of it."

She ever so slightly shook her head and silently backed herself farther into the stall. I pulled away, gave Clyde the signal in clicks and whistles, and stepped out into the open to greet the men. Taking the rag from my pocket, I wiped the grease from my hands and raked my fingers through my dirty blond hair.

"Can I help you?" I asked. Though I faced the men, I waited to hear the sound of Clyde's metal hooves stop in front of the girl's stall, effectively (or so I hoped) blocking her from their view.

"We're looking for a girl," said a tall man with a thin mustache and a pointed beard. Two men stood with him: a short man whose baldhead glistened with sweat, and a fat man whose face was red from exertion. They, too, had been running. The others casually dispersed themselves to search the stalls while the three men and I stayed in the middle near the main workbench. I counted eight men in all, and they looked strangely out of place wearing Vogue District business suits amid the Stable's machinery.

"What has she done?" I asked. The sound of Clyde's footsteps came to a stop. From the corner of my eye, I saw two men head to the back of the building, toward the girl's stall. I hoped Clyde would be enough to conceal her.

"She's run away from home," said the fat man. "Her father sent us looking for her. He's ... concerned." A slight grin passed over the men's faces, as if their comrade had hinted at an inside joke. There was more to his story than simply bringing a girl back to her father.

"What does she look like?" I asked.

"Eighteen, about your height," said the bald man, "with red hair past her shoulders. Answers to the name Rebecca." He reached into his pocket and pulled out a holophone. After pressing the touch screen a few times, a hologram image of the girl appeared floating at eye level. No doubt about it: That was the girl hiding in the back stall.

"I can't say I've seen anyone matching her description," I lied, "but I'll keep a lookout." The bald man shut off the holophone and put it back in his pocket.

"Thank you," said the man with the pointed beard. He spoke slowly and squinted his eyes, as if by looking he could catch me in my lie. But, like every child growing up in what we affectionately termed The Pits, I learned to lie before I learned to talk.

"Should you happen to see or hear anything, let us know," he continued, handing me his card. I glanced at it and noticed the Dome Corp insignia emblazoned in the center before shoving it into my pocket. I'd burn it later. He snapped his fingers twice and the group turned to leave, but they walked as slowly as possible, careful to look in every stall they passed. It wasn't until they had left the Stable and made their way a few blocks down the street that I felt it safe to return to Rebecca.

I whistled to Clyde and he stepped aside to let me enter the stall. Rebecca sat right where I'd left her, only she'd found a discarded bucket of oil and run the slick ooze through her hair to hide the red. It had mostly worked.

"So," I said, "Rebec—"

"Beka," she broke in. "My name is Beka."

"All right, Beka, would you care to explain why the Stable has suddenly become so popular?" I asked, slipping the rag back into my pocket and leaning against Clyde's shiny flank.

She stood, her posture almost regal. "I thank you for your assistance, but it's probably best for both of us if you know nothing." She stepped forward, but I blocked her path.

"I don't quite agree with that logic," I said. "It's far easier to lie for you if I know the full story."

"I didn't ask you to lie for me," she said, crossing her arms. I was surprised to see her biceps were toned, like mine. "And what makes you think you'll need to lie for me again?"

"First, you did ask me to lie for you, and second, while you don't strike me as the kind of girl to hide in the same place twice, can you really afford to turn down a potential ally?"

Her eyes searched mine. "I have nothing to offer you," she said.

"Maybe not, but I'm starving for entertainment."

"Trust me, you don't want my form of entertainment. I'd only bring you trouble." Again, she tried to walk past me and I stopped her. "Do *not* make me hurt you," she said.

"It wouldn't be the first time I've been hit by a girl. But I should warn you, I—" She shoved my arm aside, ignoring me. I let her pass. "At least stay a moment to wash the gross stuff out of your hair," I said. She kept walking. The oil dripped down her back, staining her pale green shirt and leaving glimmering black droplets on the floor. She paused only for a moment at the same door the men had left through, before heading back onto the street in the opposite direction.

As I mopped up the trail of oil, I wondered why she'd been running, and what she'd been running from. I crawled into bed that night hoping she'd found a decent place to sleep where she'd be safe.

While I cleaned the Stable the next morning, I came upon the back stall where I'd first seen Beka. She'd been so determined not to accept my help, and yet I had a feeling I might see her again. Over the next few days, I continued clearing the main stalls and rearranging everything. I made sure to leave plenty of crates, barrels and other storage containers in the last few stalls, in case Beka should show. I even threw in a few drop cloths that could be used for concealment.

Three weeks passed with no sign of Beka. I was debating whether or not I should clear out all the clutter from the last few stalls when she nearly knocked me over in her haste to enter the building. I only had a second to get my bearings before I heard a group of running feet approaching, accompanied by the sound of Beka already moving things around in her stall. I whistled a short tune and Clyde once again took his place in front of Beka's hiding place just before the men entered the Stable.

"Did you see her? Did you see the girl just now?" asked the fat man, pointing his hand in an agitated fashion.

"A group your size and you still can't find her?" I asked. "That must be some girl! Regrettably, I haven't seen her, but you're free to search the place if you like. Just don't get too close to any of the animaltrons. I haven't got around to fixing all of them yet, and they can be pretty nasty when they malfunction."

I returned to my work installing a new mechanical leg on a child's animaltron pony that had come in earlier that day, and made sure to position myself so I could maintain a clear view of Beka's stall.

The men spread out all over the Stable. I recognized most of them from their last visit, but there were more of them this time—fifteen, total—and, it occurred to me, they were old. The youngest among them seemed to be in his late forties, while the oldest was close to sixty—a bit on in years to be running all over town chasing someone my age.

I started tightening the last bolt on the animaltron pony. At the edge of my vision, I noticed the fat man approaching the back corner. A few more steps and he would be at Beka's stall.

"I wouldn't get too close, sir," I said.

He didn't stop or acknowledge me. Perhaps he'd thought I was referring to someone else. I shrugged and went back to tightening the bolt, whistling a little tune as I did so. When I stopped whistling, I was rewarded with a loud splat quickly followed by the fat man's yell.

"Ugh! What in the name of —"

I poked my head around the side of the animaltron pony to see the fat man covered from head to toe in slick, black oil. Clyde's aim was excellent, as always.

"I'm so sorry sir," I said, doing my best to sound apologetic as I walked over to him. "I tried to warn you: Clyde has a mind of his own." I grabbed a rag hanging off the side of a stall and offered it to the man, who was trying ineffectually to remove the grime from his face with his hands. He wailed with pain after accidentally rubbing oil into his eyes.

The other men made their way over to us and gathered around him. We still stood way too close to Beka's hiding place, and I didn't dare look to see if she was sufficiently hidden.

"You—! You—! You—!" the fat man yelled, jabbing his finger at me.

"I tried to warn him," I explained to the others, "but he wouldn't listen."

"That *thing* should be melted down for scrap metal and turned into a toaster!"

Stepping out of range, I gave a short whistle and watched Clyde kick the oil-slicked man in the gut. It knocked the wind out of him, sending him to the ground.

"I think it might be best to move away from the animaltrons," I said as a few of the other men rushed to help their fallen comrade. "Especially if you have any further insults."

The men nodded and muttered their "quite right"s and "yes, indeed"s as I ushered them to the front of the Stable.

"I'm terribly sorry, gentlemen," I said. "I've been no help to you at all, I'm afraid."

"You were useless! Beyond useless! This establishment is a walking death trap, and I wouldn't be surprised if it were condemned," said the fat man, throwing the rag at my feet.

"Let's move on," said one of the men. The group mumbled its assent and exited the building. I followed them to the door, waiting until they disappeared down a side street before walking to the back stall. I clicked my tongue in thanks to Clyde and whistled for him to let me pass.

"They're gone," I said. After a bit of rustling and box rearranging, Beka emerged. No one could have seen her without moving things first.

Our eyes met, and I raised an eyebrow in question.

"You were right," she said, letting out an exasperated sigh. "I could use an ally." She swung herself up onto the partition and sat, swinging her legs.

"I had a feeling you'd change your mind," I said. I pulled out a rag from my pocket and started cleaning excess oil from Clyde's backside. "But if I'm going to keep covering for you, I'm—"

"Going to want the full story," finished Beka. "I remember." She stared at me a moment. "What's your name?"

"Hans," I said.

"Hans ... as in—?"

"As in the clever horse, yes. Ironic, isn't it?"

"No, actually, I was thinking of Hans Christian Andersen, the man who wrote those ancient children's stories," she said.

I'd never heard of the guy. I merely shrugged and went back to cleaning Clyde.

"So what's a girl like you got to run away from?" I asked.

"What's that supposed to mean, a girl like me?" she asked.

"You might be wearing work clothes, but you've clearly never worked a day in your life," I said, motioning to her clean, khaki pants; white, button-down shirt, brand-new leather boots; and manicured fingers, and then pointing to my grungy, oil-stained coveralls; steel-toe boots; and calloused hands. "Vogue District girls like you aren't usually being chased all over Midtown like a criminal."

"And grungy Midtown workers like you aren't usually willing to risk their skin for Vogue District strangers. Yet here we are."

She turned her head away from me and stared at the wall. For a moment, the only sound was the faint creaking of Clyde's joints. With his backside shiny again, I tossed the grimy rag into a nearby bucket and gave him the command to go back to his usual stall. Beka turned to me. "I've decided to trust you," she said. "You've covered for me twice now, and that's good enough for me."

She hopped down off the partition and walked out into the main section of the Stable, examining my workbench but keeping her back to me. "I've been running away from my father. He ... he wants me to marry."

"That's it?" I asked. "Most girls I know have the opposite problem with their—"

"It's not like that," she said, turning to face me. "He wants me to marry this ... this ... *business* man." She said it as if it were a curse word. "He's old enough to be my *father!*" She crossed her arms and slumped down onto a nearby crate. "I told my father I wouldn't, I *couldn't*, marry someone like that, but he just ..."

Her fingertips drew back her hair from her face and brushed over a small scar on her cheek I hadn't noticed before. I understood. Growing up in The Pits, I have my fair share of similar scars.

"That was the first day I ran away," she continued. "The servants found me in little over an hour and brought me back, but the next day, I slipped out again. I've gotten better. It takes them longer and longer to find me. My record so far is three days. It would have been longer only the baker ratted me out. I guess I deserved it after eating two loaves of bread, a dozen cookies and a slice of cake from her storeroom."

"Pig," I teased. She smirked at me. "So if your father has money to pay servants to chase after you, why does he send them after you on foot? Every cop in the area at least has a hover scooter or something."

"My father's cheap, though he prefers to call it 'frugal,'" she said. "One of the servants suggested they insert a tracking chip in me, but thankfully, Father believes that if his men can consistently bring me back, he can avoid spending money on some silly device."

We talked for a while longer. As the hours dragged on, I went into the small living quarters adjacent to the Stable, which consisted of a bed, bathroom and tiny kitchen, and managed to retrieve something close to a meal from my meager store.

"The bread's stale, the cheese is a little moldy, and the apples are bruised, but it's, well, edible," I said lamely, setting down the food and taking a seat next to Beka on a large crate. I grabbed the small loaf of bread and broke it in half, offering the larger of the two to Beka.

"Believe me, nothing can be worse than the stuff I stole from the Midtown grocer's trash bin last week," said Beka, taking the bread, her fingers softly brushing against mine.

"You didn't..."

"Well, I was hungry, and it looked close to edible!" The bread crunched as she broke off a piece and popped it in her mouth.

"Everyone knows that even the stuff he *sells* isn't entirely edible," I explained.

"Well, I guess it's a good thing I've got you to warn me about these things now." She bit into one of the apples and I couldn't help but notice it was the same color as her lips.

Around sunset, Beka made some excuse about not wanting to stay in one place for too long and left. Though she couldn't say when, she promised she'd be back, and I found myself looking forward to her visit. In fact, I couldn't get her out of my mind.

True to her word, two weeks later, on a cold, winter evening, she snuck into the Stable. I was refurbishing an old hover sleigh I'd salvaged from the junkyard, and nearly burned myself with my welding torch when she tapped my shoulder. No one had caught sign of her trail yet, so she was in no hurry to conceal herself. Just the same, I gave Clyde the signal to guard the front door.

"How do you do that?" she asked.

"Do what?" I said. I finished welding a piece of paneling on the hover sleigh, turned off the blowtorch, and removed my visor.

"You make those noises and he just ... responds. I've never seen an animaltron do such a thing."

"That's because Clyde is the only animaltron that can. At least, that I know of. I programmed him for it. It's easy enough to learn. You want to try it?"

She nodded, her eyes scrutinizing the hover sleigh. I sifted through all the clutter on my workbench and pulled out the cheat sheet I'd made two years ago when I first programmed Clyde to respond to clicks and whistles.

"The whole communication system relies on Morse code," I explained, handing her the sheet. "Each dot represents a click, and each dash represents a whistle. Initially, I would spell everything out but that took too long, so I came up with shorthand. Try this one." I pointed to the letter "S" on the chart, which had three dots next to it.

Beka clicked her tongue three times, and Clyde obediently stepped forward.

That was the first time I saw Beka smile, and it made her even more beautiful. The warmth of her smile spread out from around her, warming the cold, drafty Stable.

I guided her through the basic commands: walk, run, turn, halt, guard, and so on. Then I had her give Clyde a series of commands which led him around the Stable and right up to the hover sleigh I'd finished repairing. I walked over and began hitching him to the harness.

The hover sleigh was designed to look like its antique counterpart in terms of shape, only instead of red-painted wood, the whole thing was made of steel. Where the front of the antique version just had an empty space for one's feet, the front of this one more closely resembled the cockpit of one of those airplanes on display in the museum. There were gauges and dials to monitor the engine and rocket boosters, and various switches that I could reprogram for my own devices.

"You want to go for a ride?" I asked Beka as I finished with Clyde's harness.

"On your sleigh? No, I couldn't."

"C'mon, I have to take it for a test drive, anyway."

"What if someone sees me?"

"No one will see you. Not the way we're going," I said. "You trust me, right?"

She nodded. "And you're sure we won't be seen?"

"Positive." I climbed into the sleigh, suddenly aware how tattered the seat cushions looked, and held out my hand to help her in. She looked out the door of the Stable. It was dark outside, and a light, artificial snow had begun to fall. The only light came from the buildings lining the narrow street outside. She turned back to me and placed her hand in mine.

"All right," she said, "but I swear, if you get me captured, so help me, I will strangle you."

"Duly noted." With the push of a button, I started up the hover sleigh, and it slowly lifted off the ground, about a foot in the air. Clyde guided us out onto the street, not a single person in sight to watch as his torso opened, and he extended his wings. I kicked the boosters into high gear, and we slowly rose farther into the air, hovering above the rooftops, higher than any hover car could fly.

"See, I told you no one would be able to see you," I said. We briefly circled over Midtown, where the Stable and most of the smaller shops stood, before I guided Clyde to the center of the Dome, toward Downtown's skyscrapers, which nearly punctured the zenith of the force field.

"It's so beautiful," said Beka, her hand outstretched to catch the faux snowflakes. "I wish I could stay up here forever."

"I know the feeling," I said. She caught me staring at her, and I quickly looked away. "So, this thing with your father; has he always been so controlling?"

"He wasn't always. Things used to be fine, but ever since his promotion to weather manager at Dome Corp he's been different. All he cares about is how much money he makes. Signing away his daughter's freedom in some arranged marriage is nothing more than a money-making scheme."

"Can't you convince him otherwise?" I asked.

"My own mother can't even sway him." She looked down at the twinkling lights of the city below us as we approached Downtown. "If I had things my way, I'd run away from here and never come back; go somewhere where my father would never find me. Somewhere I could be free."

"You could try the women's bath house. He'll never look for you there," I said.

She playfully punched my shoulder. "Hans, be serious."

"I am serious. He's only sending men after you, so naturally--"

The rest of my sentence dissolved as we broke into laughter. The thought of her father's men, red-faced with embarrassment, attempting to follow Beka through the bathhouse was too comical.

"You are ridiculous," she said as our laughs subsided. She leaned against my shoulder and gazed up at the false image of the sky.

"I've always wondered what it would be like outside the Dome," I said, as I glanced up at the projection of the moon through the fake snow. "See what the real sky looks like, and if everything out there is as dangerous as Dome Corp claims it is."

"You don't believe them?"

I shook my head. "First chance I get, I'm leaving the Dome, to see the outside world for myself. I mean, can we really believe anything they tell us? They control everything—even the weather."

"Not everything." She smiled and entwined her fingers in mine. "They can't control rebels like us."

* * *

Though Beka never came around on the same day or at the same time, she came regularly enough that I began to expect her at least twice a week, if not more, so I was surprised when I didn't see her for a week. At the time, I figured it was just Beka trying to be unpredictable and shrugged it off, but after another week passed without a glimpse of her, I grew concerned. On the twentieth day, I was debating whether or not I should go look for her when she burst into the Stable with an uncharacteristically loud entrance, slamming the door shut behind her.

I'd never seen her look so frantic. Or such a mess. Her hair was so tangled, either from running or lack of brushing, it was matted in places. Her clothes, usually pristine, were caked with mud.

"What happened t--"

"No time to explain," she said, cutting me off. "I've got to leave the Dome, now!"

"What? Why?" I asked. She started pacing around the Stable, flitting from one stall to the next, not knowing whether to hide or keep pacing.

"Remember how I told you Father was too cheap to do the whole tracking chip thing?"

"Yeah."

"That stupid *businessman* talked him into it once he got wind of my runaway habit. The only way Father could seal the arranged wedding was to promise I'd be chipped next week!" "When will they chip you?"

"Saturday," she said. "I overheard Father arranging everything."

"Damn!" I, too, began pacing. One week was hardly enough time for all we'd have to accomplish. I glanced around the Stable, searching for inspiration, and my eyes landed on the hover sleigh. A plan started forming in my mind.

"I've got something," I said. "It's crazy and risky, but, if we do it right, it should get us out of the Dome."

"Us?" asked Beka. "You'll come with me?"

"I'm not about to let you have all the fun," I said. Beka ran toward me and nearly tackled me with a hug that squeezed the air out of my lungs. At that moment, it was the best feeling in the world.

I pulled out an old, dusty map and some paper, and laid them across the crate we used as our table. Beka had seen the maps in her father's office enough to know that there were still a few cities outside Dome Corp's control, and these she had marked on our map. The closest was Diova, a small town about a hundred miles away. That would be our first destination. From there, we would decide our next move.

Getting out of the Dome itself was going to be trickier. The few people Beka knew working the gates were too closely allied to her father for them to be much help to her, and the one guy I knew wasn't big on favors. I'd probably have to bribe him.

A week wasn't quite long enough to make many changes to the hover sleigh, but a few days would give me time to sync its programming with Clyde's. If I skimped on sleep I could probably even up the speed a little, but I didn't mention this to Beka. I didn't want to get her hopes up. She'd have to play the good girl and sit at home for the next few days to avoid suspicion, so it would be up to me to make all the preparations. Between provisions, bribing the guard and upgrades to Clyde and the sleigh, I was going to have my hands full.

Finalizing our plans took a few hours, and the artificial sun was beginning to set across the Dome when I finally convinced Beka to head back to Vogue District.

"Friday night, midnight," I reminded her. "We'll meet here and I'll have everything ready for us."

"I'll be here," she said, stepping closer to me.

"Whatever you do, don't arouse suspicion."

"I won't."

"And don't let anyone follow you."

"Hans."

"Because if something happened to you, I—"

Beka placed a smooth finger over my lips. Her touch distracted me so much, I forgot what I was going to say. "I'll be careful," she whispered. She took my hands in hers, leaned in, and kissed me. She was warm, and soft, and I could taste the salt of her sweat on her lips. I felt like I was hovering, and in that moment, with our arms wrapped around each other, nothing seemed impossible.

The next few days flew by, and I never had enough time. I found myself falling asleep at my workbench each night instead of making it to my bed. I don't even remember if I ate.

By the time Friday arrived, I was more crazed than Beka when she'd last run into the Stable. I'd secured passage out of the Dome, but it took all my savings to bribe the guard. Our timing would have to be perfect; the guard's partner must go on break before we would come through. And we must not be seen. Even with a head start, anyone with a decent hover car would catch up to us in 25 miles. No amount of tweaking could make Clyde or the hover sleigh go much faster. If we wanted to make it out alive, we *couldn't* be followed.

At sunset, I loaded the hover sleigh with our provisions. By 9 p.m., I was ready to leave and I couldn't sit still. I went through every stall, making sure I'd packed what we'd need. I checked the hover sleigh multiple times, to be certain the gear was secure. I checked the engines, the oil, Clyde's circuitry. By 10 p.m., I had quadruple-checked everything. I would drive myself insane if I checked everything again, so instead I climbed the ladder to the Stable's attic loft. From a small window, I could see the view of Midtown below and

Vogue District rising on the hill beyond. A small Vogue District light blinked irregularly. No, not irregularly: it blinked in Morse code. I pulled a pen from my pocket and, having nothing else to write on, began translating the words onto the wall. I kept writing until the letter sequence repeated itself. The message read:

HANS. LOCKED IN ROOM. NO WAY OUT. HELP. BEKA.

I flew down the ladder so fast, I tripped over the rungs. How long had she been signaling? I rummaged around the hover sleigh until I found my flashlight and raced back up the ladder to the window. I only had time for one word:

COMING.

I don't remember how I got to her mansion. She'd pointed it out to me from the hover sleigh once, but down on the ground I had difficulty locating it. I didn't dare ask anyone for directions, lest they be added to a list of witnesses who could identify me. It took nearly half an hour, but I finally found Beka's place nestled against the edge of the Dome's force field among similarly huge estates. Despite the size of the mansions, the slope of the overarching force field made everything feel small and cramped.

Perfectly manicured lawns and bushes surrounded Beka's dome-roofed mansion. Rich as they were, these people didn't find fencing necessary. They had far more sophisticated ways of keeping trespassers out. I poked around the bushes until I found the front yard's security panel. In a matter of seconds, I pulled out my multi-tool from my pocket, popped off the security panel's protective covering, and, with a bit of rewiring, deactivated the security sensors.

An electric-blue glow coming from the second-story window caught my eye. The window was encased in a crisscrossing net of electric currents. I silently thanked Beka's father for making the location of his daughter's room so obvious.

Cautiously, I slipped around the side of the house and located the servants' entrance. I readied to hack the keypad lock, but heard a loud voice on the other side of the door. A large bush stood against the wall to my right, and I dove behind it, hiding in the shadows just as a servant woman came through the door, singing and carrying a bag of trash. With such a heavy load, she neglected to close the door all the way, so the second she turned, I slipped into the house.

I found myself in a small service room. The servants had hung their coats on hooks along the wall to my right. To my left was a closet. If I went any farther, someone would notice I didn't belong, but I couldn't stay put, either. The servant woman would be back any minute.

I opened the closet to find it full of spare linens, towels and servants' uniforms. I grabbed a uniform and started to undress, but I heard the servant woman singing outside the door. Quickly, I shut myself in the closet and held my breath, waiting. The door opened and the woman walked across the room. When the sound of her footsteps faded, I changed into the uniform: black dress pants, a button-down shirt and a vest. I rescued my multi-tool and flashlight from the heap of clothes on the floor, and shoved them into the pockets of the dress pants, then casually walked down the hallway

After several wrong turns, I found the grand staircase in the main entryway of the house. I climbed as fast as I dared, cringing at the tiniest noise. My servant uniform wouldn't help me if someone caught me using this stairway instead of the servant's hall.

Once I reached the landing, I turned right. Her room was easy to spot because two servants stood guard in front of a door next to a control panel for a bio-lock mechanism. Only the retina of someone with proper security clearance could unlock it.

I tried to act cool as I approached, my heart racing.

"You the new guy, Mitch?" asked one of the guards. His booming voice made me jump.

"Yes," I lied.

"About time! What took you so long?"

"Bathroom."

"Ty will relieve you next. Miss has already had her dinner. Don't let her convince you otherwise. I'm off now."

He left, but the giant boulder of a man next to me didn't acknowledge my presence. In fact, he hadn't moved or spoken during my entire exchange with the other guard.

A yell of frustration burst from the other side of the door. No doubt about it: Beka was locked inside, and from the sound of it, there was no easy escape. I needed to find a way to communicate with her. I glanced up at the guard. He stared straight ahead, not even blinking, so I began whistling a tune and tapping a beat on the door behind me. I tapped randomly at first, but after the guard made no objections, I switched to Morse code.

I'M HERE. 1 GUARD. IDEAS?

I kept whistling, but I stopped tapping. I only hoped the guard wouldn't notice which side of the door the tapping came from. It took a few seconds before Beka tapped back:

BE READY.

Then she shouted, "Whoever's out there, stop the whistling and tapping and open up. I need to use the bathroom."

I looked at the guard and raised a brow. He sighed, turned to the bio-lock mechanism, and held his eye up to the scanner. A blue beam of light scanned his retina. With a quiet beep, the door slid open, and Beka attacked, thumping the guard on the head. With a soft thud, he collapsed, unconscious. I stared, dumbfounded.

"How'd you do that?" I asked.

She held up an antique book with yellowed pages. "I'd always told my father I didn't want his old book collection in my room," she said. "I guess it can stay after all."

We pulled the guard into her room and closed the door so it stood open just a crack in case we needed to get out that way. "What's the plan?" she asked.

"Window?"

"High-voltage electric currents. The control panel is on the wall next to it, but the pass code changes daily, if not hourly. I've tried to crack the code multiple times with no luck."

"Other exit options?"

"No good ones. We'll probably be seen no matter which way we go," she said.

I walked over to the window's control panel and removed the protective front piece, exposing the mainframe and the wiring. This was far more sophisticated than the security system I'd disarmed in the front yard. If I cut the wrong wire or entered the wrong code, the alarm would trigger, and we'd be discovered. But if we went out through any of the main doors of the house, we risked being seen.

"Can we use another window?" I asked.

Beka shook her head. "No. My father locked all the other rooms along this hall. An alarm will sound if anyone enters them."

"Then we only have one option," I said. I pulled the multi-tool from my pocket. "I'm going to disarm the electric currents, but in order to do it, I'll have to trigger the alarm. You ready to jump?"

"Hold on." Beka ran to her closet and pulled out a rope made of clothes and bed sheets, which she tied to her dresser. She left the coiled end near the window, then slung a small backpack over her shoulder. "What? You didn't think I'd just sit here waiting, did you?"

I pulled one of the wires, and a loud siren immediately assaulted my eardrums. I pulled another wire, but that only made the electric current stronger.

"Hans!" shouted Beka, plugging her ears.

"I'm trying!"

I pulled another wire, and the horizontal currents disappeared, but amid the screech of the siren, I could hear the distant sound of shouts and running feet.

"Hans, they're coming!"

I cut another wire, with no effect.

Beka snatched the multi-tool from my hand, and cut the bundle of wires in one shot. The remaining bars of electricity ceased. She immediately threw the makeshift rope out the window and began climbing down just as the door opened.

I turned to see the man with the pointed beard.

"You!" he shouted. I hurried to the window and leapt over the ledge as quickly as I could, but I misjudged the distance between it and the bushes below, landing half in a bush and half on the lawn.

"Move! Move!" urged Beka. She pulled me to my feet, and we raced down the front lawn, out onto the street. Beka knew all the back alleys around her neighborhood. I followed her as close as I could, but she nearly lost me with the tight, sudden turns and strange obstacles. Running down a narrow alley between two buildings and snaking through trashcans, we finally leapt over the walls of a short shrubbery maze in someone's backyard, where an animaltron dog chased us across the lawn. Three more blocks brought us to the Stable.

Out of breath, we burst through the door and headed for Clyde and the hover sleigh. Beka leapt in immediately. "Here, put this on," I said, handing her a helmet equipped with an integrated comms system.

"I didn't need one of these before," she said warily.

"I made a few adjustments," I said. "Put it on and strap yourself in."

"Hans, how fast will this thing go?"

"Not fast enough," I said. I climbed in and started up the engines as we donned our helmets.

With the hum of the engines came a stampede of footsteps. I whistled Clyde's signal, sending him into autopilot and activating his pre-programmed route. We began to exit the building, but just as we approached the Stable doors, so did the men. There were too many to count, and this time, they'd come armed.

"Give us the girl and we'll let you live!" shouted the fat man. I flipped a few levers on the hover sleigh, splattering the mob with oil. Clyde sped up, pushing aside the first group of men, but more of them gathered beyond the Stable doors, and they weren't impaired by lubricants. Within seconds, they swarmed the sleigh.

The men grabbed for us, trying to pull us out. One guy grabbed my leg, only to get kicked in the face a moment later. I had just punched another guy off the sleigh when I heard Beka scream through her comms unit. I turned – one of the men had latched onto Beka's legs while she desperately clung to the back of her seat. Without thinking, I lunged for the man, tackling him to the ground. The fall knocked the air out of him, temporarily incapacitating him. I turned to climb back into the sleigh only to realize that it had begun its ascent as we were fighting.

Beka's voice came through my helmet: "Hans! Get in!" I made a jump for the runners of the hover sleigh, grabbing on with my right hand.

Unfortunately, the men in the crowd had the exact same idea. Those who hadn't managed to grab a hold of the sleigh runners grabbed for my legs and started to pull. With the added weight, the hover sleigh started to sink back to the ground. I kicked the man holding me and managed to shake him off, but another came in his place. Meanwhile, Beka did serious damage with a wrench, breaking the fingers of the men trying to stop us. They wailed before falling to the crowd below, flattening those they landed on.

My right arm ached from the strain. I tried to kick the man grabbing my ankles, but I merely swung him into the head of another man in the crowd. I attempted to reach my left arm up to grab onto the runner, but the man pulled me down and my right arm lacked the strength to lift me the slightest bit farther.

"Hans! Look out!" shouted Beka. But her warning came too late. One of the men who had managed to escape Beka's wrench came up on my right side and kicked me in the gut. My hand let go of the runner and I fell, landing in the crowd below. A moment later, the man who'd kicked me fell to the ground, a bloody gash across his forehead.

I hurried to get on my feet, but the men grabbed my arms and legs. The man with the pointed beard held a gun to my head and called up to Beka, who was now alone on the hover sleigh.

"Come back down and we'll let this boy go!" he said.

"Don't listen to him!" I said into the comms unit. "Get out of here!"

Clyde was still on autopilot. She'd be safe if she just stayed on the hover sleigh. I watched her gaze shift from me to my captor. The hover sleigh paused in the air, and, for a moment, it appeared to descend. But within seconds, the boosters kicked in, and the sleigh began to move forward. I saw the look of panic in Beka's eyes.

"No! Stop!"

She tried to whistle for Clyde to halt, but he wouldn't respond, not without the override command. She looked back. The hover sleigh picked up speed and began to pull her out of sight. The men bound me and dragged me off, but Beka's voice echoed in my helmet.

Between the static and her tears, I heard her promise: "I'll come for you."

Dashing Through the Snow

By Maggie Marr

"I hate snow!" Ella Brighton yelled as she stomped on the brake of her gargantuan SUV. With every fiber of her being, she willed her rental to stop. Her ten perfectly manicured nails dug into the faux-leather steering wheel. Finally--finally after one hundred yards her elephantine truck slid to a stop in the center of an intersection.

Vermont was a death trap.

Sure, some people thought the white stuff was fun and cute even playful, but snow was silent death. The idea that something solid and cold (cold enough to kill you) fell from the sky and created monoliths that giant truck had to forcibly remove so that civilized people could drive? Those thoughts terrified Ella. Snow was like an alligator dressed up in a kitten costume.

She glanced over at Bovis, heavily lidded and unimpressed, as he lay on the passenger seat. All giant ears and a puddle of drool, the dog truly resembled Brad, Ella's ex-husband.

"Ah, my sweet Bovis, I may have to sell the house, but at least I got you." Ella punched at the GPS encouraging the sociopathic female voice that soothed and yet taunted to bring forth some magic instruction as to where the hell she was located. Instead, while Ella fiddled with it in the middle of the intersection, her windows fogged up. Great, not only was she lost and unable to drive, but she couldn't see. She lowered both her and Bovis' windows to let the moisture dissipate.

Bovis, so used to the warm L.A. climate, perked up his long, limp ears. His nose slowly turned toward the window, and he lumbered onto his four feet and sniffed the air. The sniff of a true dog. The sniff of a hound dog deep in the Vermont woods. A hound dog bred generation after generation for hunting and treeing and tracking, but who had spent his entire life in a city with cars and cats and sirens. Bovis, in that moment, caught his very first true sniff of life, and the dog who'd never in all his years of captivity had any urge to do much of anything, but do his business and lay around on the couch watching sports (again, much like her ex-husband, Brad) did the most terrible of terribles: With freedom at his paw tips, he decided to run.

As if a gazelle and not a lazy hound dog, Bovis leaped out the window and into a snowdrift at the side of the SUV. He disappeared from view and Ella's heart clutched with fear.

"Bovis!" she yelled. Unbelievable. This horrible behavior was so uncharacteristic. She leaned across her now-empty Starbucks cup and tried to peer out the window. "You get back in here now!"

He didn't listen.

Ella was left with one choice: Leave the dog? For an instant, the thought floated through her mind, suspended like a helium balloon, but then burst with the pinprick of realization that she needed Bovis because—as pathetic as it sounded—he was the only thing left in her life to love.

Ella carefully maneuvered the SUV out of the roadway, rolled up the windows, and turned off the ignition. She looked at her feet. Yes, she wore boots. She grew up in Chicago and understood winter—however her boots were not equipped for Vermont. These were brand-new, black leather boots with heels. Good-looking for her arrival at the Christmas Eve cocktail reception which by now she'd be lucky to make.

Why not Christmas in Tahiti? Or if her sister Lily was set on staying on this side of the world, perhaps Cabo? Anything but Vermont.

With a grumble, Ella pushed open the door. She shivered as the cold rushed through her jacket and kissed her skin. She hated Bovis for putting her through this; the snow, the cold, the silence—the scenery. She pulled on her hat and slammed the door shut. She would find him and then—she would kill him.

"Bovis!" Ella yelled as she traipsed around the back of the truck toward the spot where he made his leap to freedom. Tracks, yes. Bovis, no. How could he have disappeared so fast? He was old and slow. She never would have guessed he had a hurdle jump left in him.

She cupped her hands around her mouth, "Bovis!"

She waited, surrounded by deathly silence and the nothingness of a blanket of white. Only the skeleton limbs of trees broke up the cold palette. Giant tears threatened to spill forth. What could she do? How could she find him? Why had he left her? Her bottom lip trembled as she contemplated the giant snowdrift in front of her, a drift that contained Bovis' tracks. She looked out beyond through the trees hoping to see the tip of a tail, a dangly ear, even a huge poo. Nothing.

"Dammit, Bovis, we live in LA!"

Ella puckered her lip and thrust her gloved hands into the pockets of her coat. The night was gray from the eerie light of fresh snow reflected back against the low clouds. She yelled again, but heard only the echo of her voice. Eventually, she'd have to go back to the car. She longed for the warmth of the heater. She even longed for her sister and the fire that surely burned at the cabin. Who was she kidding? To leave Bovis was to kill him. She hadn't meant what she thought earlier. Sure this little romp might be adventurous now, maybe even fun (much like a Laker Girl after seven years of marriage), but what would happen once his itty-bitty paws grew numb and his tummy became hungry? Then what would he do? Hmm? He'd crawl right back to her ... the woman with a graduate degree and a long-term investment plan.

Ella called once more and wrapped her arms around her body. This, Bovis leaving her, wasn't about Brad so why did she have to put her entire life in the context of her ex-husband? Past and present? She chewed on her bottom lip and cocked an eyebrow. Any woman was better off without a cheating bastard than with one. But with Brad (at least in the beginning) there had been love and companionship and support. They'd gotten each other through grad school, the start of their careers, and the purchase of their first two homes. They'd even gotten each other through innumerable rounds of IVF, with the final round proving more fatal than fertile—at least to their marriage.

"Bovis, please come back!" She begged, her throat soar from the cold. Numbness nipped at her fingers and toes. Ella was surprised at how similar the numbness in her body felt to the numbness caused by divorce.

The rapid descent of lethal precipitation, quickly filled Bovis' tracks. Teardrops rolled out Ella's eyes. Her breath tightened at the prospect of losing sight of her car. She spun around and peered through the trees. Where was it? Her stomach dropped to her toes. Big, thick flakes obscured her vision. Death by frozen fluff. Ella clenched her jaw and set her stride. If she escaped from the winter clutch of her family's beloved Chicago seventeen years before; she could definitely outwit the white stuff in Vermont.

Once she spotted the car, the sunshine of satisfaction spread across her face. She'd sit in the SUV, warm up, try once more for cell reception (like throwing a pebble in a canyon) and then she'd head to the cabin. It had to be close; she guessed less than a mile from that very spot. Once there she'd find someone—anyone to help her begin again her search for Bovis.

Finally back to the SUV, Ella pulled up on the door handle. She anxiously anticipated the warmth from the heater once she turned the key in the ignition, but—the door didn't open.

She shook her head, her smile still plastered on her face. One had to find humor even in tragic situations. *Of course* she locked the doors even in *snowstorm* in Vermont in the middle of *nowhere.* To lock a door in a big city was an automatic reflex. Home, car, bathroom, garage, every door got locked—well, unless you were Brad and banging a Laker girl—then why not leave your office door wide open?

She reached in her right coat pocket for the car key. Empty. A trickle of anxiousness laced through her chest. She shoved her hands into her coat pockets and furiously searched ... *nothing*? Nothing! Panic rushed through her. She checked her jean pockets, each side, back. Then, coat once again.

She cupped her hands against the driver-side window, and pressed her nose to the chilled glass. Even through the grayish dark, she could see the plastic keychain attached to her rental car keys. Oh good, it glowed in the dark. That helped.

"No. Way." Fear bit through Ella. A type of fear she'd not experienced: terror. Her mind rushed through every Discovery survival show had had halfheartedly watched with Brad; Survivor Man, Bear What's-His-Name. Unless she could take down a moose, slice it open, and climb inside for warmth, she didn't' have a prayer.

Ella walked around the SUV, testing each door handle—not once, not twice, but three times. She even tried the back hatch. Who wanted to be the fatality in that newspaper article: "She unwittingly froze to death without the knowledge that her back hatch door was unlocked." Somehow, her family wouldn't be surprised.

No phone. No keys. No food. No dog.

"What am I going to do!" she yelled to no one, to

anyone. She was doing to die, that's what she was going to do. She read *Into the Wild*, even saw the movie. What about Jack Kerouac's *To Build a Fire*? She hadn't fallen into any water, but she didn't have any matches, either. Truly, she had absolutely no survival skills, not one. Did she build a snow cave and crawl inside, or walk down the road in an attempt to find a place with warmth? The news article again (as though her death would be news) flashed through her mind: "Los Angeles woman found frozen to death a mere ten minutes from Denny's."

She would walk. She would stay on the road and she would walk, at least for a while. She wouldn't walk so far that she couldn't get back, but she needed to see, to check if perhaps there was a pot of black coffee and a Grand Slam breakfast just beyond the giant evergreens.

After trudging through the snow Ella realized there was no pot of coffee, no warmth, no driveways or turn-offs or *lights, and definitely no Grand Slam.* In fact, aside from the road, there was no sign of civilization. Her hands were frozen and her feet hurt, she'd never wear these boots again after tonight. She had no idea of the time. Her watch waited in her car, in her purse, ticking away. Her flight had landed at 7 p.m. Then it was a 90-minute drive, and she thought she'd nearly been to the cabin when Bovis made his getaway. The time had to be, what--nearing midnight?

Perhaps she needed to consider building a snow cave. She scanned the wood on either side of the road. Did she merely pick a drift and dig? What were the requirements of a life-saving snow cave for one? Ella clasped her hands together to say a prayer for: a) her life, and b) a sign on where to build her cave, when she heard a sound like an angel's voice.

"Woof!"

"Bovis?" Ella was uncertain from which direction the bark came because while traipsing through this frozen hell the winter night had turned black as ink.

"Woof! Woof!"

"Where are you?" She asked beneath her breath as she spun from side to side.

"Boooooovis!" she yelled with every ounce of need, want, and pain. If she was going to freeze to death on Christmas Eve, at least let her do it with her dog. She plowed forward and turned down a bend in the road. There, barely visible in the moonlight sitting high like a prince on a throne, was her beloved Bovis.

"Is that you, boy?" Perhaps dehydration or hypothermia caused hallucinations for where had Bovis found a sleigh, a team of two horses and—hello—she hoped the hallucination was real: a hot cowboy.

"Whoa!" the cowboy called as he pulled back on the

reins and both chestnut-colored horses came to a docile stop beside her. Ella gazed up at the handsome man in the sleigh, and a single realization coursed through her: She would know this man well. She fought the urge to rush to him and touch him with a familiarity that seeped through her.

Bovis leaped from the sleigh, his joy palpable, and pulled the two humans from their locked gaze. The dog landed in front of Ella. He stood on his hind legs and placed his front paws on each of Ella's shoulders as he licked her frozen tears.

"Oh, Bovis, you scared me." Ella settled her forehead against his, and for once, didn't' care about drool on her jacket. Bovis was safe, and he'd rescued her from certain death. He swiped his tongue up the side of her face. Rescue dog or not, sloppy, drooly kisses were not her thing.

"Love you, buddy," Ella said as she ran the back of her glove over her slobbered face and then scratched the dog behind his ears. Now fully aware of Bovis' penchant for freedom, Ella held firm his collar and patted his head.

"You must be Ella," the cowboy said. Relieved to see Bovis and not to feel the clutches of sudden death she turned her gaze back to the gorgeous guy in the sleigh.

And you must be the best Christmas present ever.

"Excuse me?" the Cowboy leaned forward, and laugh lines danced around his eyes.

"Wait? What? I'm Ella," she said, horrified that perhaps in her state of hypothermic dementia she actually muttered her words out loud.

"Sorry," he said, and slid his hand across the front of his cowboy hat. "I thought you mentioned something about the best Christmas present ever."

Oops. She did say it out loud. But, wow what girl didn't want a cowboy under her Christmas tree, and one that had saved her life?

"How do you know who I am and where I am and—"

"Ma'am, it's all because of Bovis." He tied the reins, flicked on two spotlights on the front of the sleigh, and then climbed down from his seat. He was tall and solid and everything Ella believed a man should be, but had somehow forgotten while drowning in a sea of metrosexuals. As he approached and stepped into the light, his blue eyes sparkled. The plain of his cheeks beneath sharp cheekbones begged to be touched. Ella fought the urge to pull off her glove and let her numb fingertips dance across his solid jaw.

"You are—?" Ella whispered, unable to keep breath in her body with him suddenly so near.

"I'm Jake."

Butterflies couldn't survive winter, but Ella's insides fluttered. From forsaken to found. She felt her knees tremble. She had her dog, a gorgeous man that she hoped was going to take her someplace warm, and a ... a ... sleigh?

"Hey, there, pretty lady, you okay?" Jake reached out and steadied Ella with his strong arms. "I got your name off your dog's tags."

She looked into Jake's eyes. "Just relieved ... I mean, I thought I was going to die."

"Die?" Jake asked, as if he hadn't heard her right. He fought to keep the grin off his face and the laughter from his voice.

Anger rapidly replaced lust and she found the strength in her legs and considered pulling herself away from his grasp.

"I lost my dog, as you know, and locked my keys in my car. I've been walking for what seems like hours, and it's like twenty below zero. A person could freeze to death out here!"

Jake nodded, a smile forming. "I'm awful glad I found you then." He bent forward, and in one strong swoop, lifted Ella from the treacherous snow. "Let's get you back to the cabin."

She settled into the sleigh next to him.

"Come on, Bovis!" he called, and the dog jumped into the back row of the sleigh, his head between them. Jake tucked a red, plaid blanket over her legs. "I'll send a couple men for your car. They'll get the door open and drive it back." He lifted a silver Thermos. "Hot cocoa?"

Warmth shot through her at the sight of Jake's full smile and, well, the blanket and hot cocoa, helped, too. She went from potentially the worst night of her life to possibly one of the best.

"So do you work at the resort?" She clasped tight the cup of hot cocoa, the heat warming her fingertips. Once he stowed the Thermos, Jake gently tapped the reins on the rumps of the horses, and they turned the sleigh around.

"Now, that's a tricky question."

Great. The effervescent bubbles of lust she felt suddenly landed like a solid lump of wet, dirty laundry. She'd heard every excuse a man could make about every *tricky question* that a suspicious wife might ask. She pursed her lips and settled in to hear what a cowboy in Vermont might consider "tricky."

"I do work at the resort, but that's because I own the cabins, the main house and about three thousand acres of land around it."

So much for tricky. There had to be a catch: a rich, good-looking cowboy? Perhaps he was married there was no way for her to tell since he wore gloves. Besides since when was a wedding ring an accurate litmus test for determining whether a man was married?

Ella rested her hand on Bovis' head and decided to fish. "All that land plus your family must keep you busy."

"It did, I mean it does. Just me in Vermont, anymore. I have a brother in Atlanta, one in LA, and, well," Jake paused and Ella saw a twitch in his jaw. "An ex-wife in Maine."

"I'm sorry."

"Don't be. Was the best thing that could have happened for either of us." Jake gently tapped the reins, requesting the horses to pick up the pace. "What about you?"

Ella heard genuine interest in Jake's voice with his question. His face, with its smile lines creasing the corners of his amazing eyes and kissable mouth, appeared to delight in anticipation of her response. Her heart lifted. How long had it been since she actually felt something other than simply sexual interest from a man? She guessed years—nearly a decade."

"Same," Ella barely contained the lilt in her voice. "I mean, no brother in Atlanta and while I live in Los Angeles, the rest of my family, including my sister, Lily, who you might have met at the ranch, live in Chicago." She didn't want to ramble, but she couldn't seem to halt the torrent of drivel that escaped her lips. Didn't men hate rambling women? Women making noise, noise, noise, in their attempt at conversation. Wasn't that just nails on a chalkboard for any man? Ella took a deep breath and allowed herself one final statement. "When I say 'the same,' I mean divorced. I'm divorced. It's been nearly two years."

"So your wounds a little fresher than mine," Jake said without looking away from the road and the gently falling giant flakes. If she had to admit it, the gorgeous cowboy beside her appeared beautiful and soft, as if an emissary of peace.

He turned and fixed his brilliant blue eyes on her. "I promise," he said, his voice deep as if making a solemn vow, "it gets better."

She realized in the logical part of her brain that Jake was right because with each passing day she became a little less broken and a little more sane. But then, there were moments when the thoughts of all that was lost by Brad's infidelity sank their teeth deep in her soul. Those days were fewer and further. But even now, two years later she still felt exposed, naked, vulnerable, as if she could not trust her own sense to keep her safe. She'd failed so miserably once; how could she ever trust her judgment about a man?

"Infidelity is a horrible thing," Jake said, as if climbing into her mind and reading her thoughts. Again, she wondered, if she ruminated out loud. "My wife ... well, she felt awful alone." His voice softened, and while the outline of a smile still decorated his face, the hints of sadness surrounded his eyes. "I was out chasing dollars, and someone I thought was a good friend starting chasing her."

The weight of Jake's statement, his honesty, his own

choice at vulnerability pressed into Ella's chest. He, too, had felt the betrayal, the anger, the rejection, yet here he sat beside her, sharing his tale. He wasn't embarrassed by the loss of his wife and his marriage; it was a part of his story. A part that Ella knew just by his tone and the set of his jaw.

"My husband," Ella started and stopped. Had she ever really said the word aloud? No, not even to her family or her therapist. She danced around cloaked words, as if a ballerina on a stage of broken glass. "My *ex*-husband had an affair."

Ella finally said it. The weightlessness that wafted through her chest with the release of the word over her lips shocked her.

And she giggled. She clamped her gloved hand over her mouth. *How inappropriate, especially after Jake shared his very own heartbreak.*

Jake looked over and cocked an eyebrow. "That's funny?" he asked, with a hint of humor in his voice.

Ella looked into his eyes. "It hasn't been, at least not until now."

Jake nodded, and his face broke into a full smile. "It's a good sign when you laugh. It shows you're ready to move on. Means you've turned that corner from rage, which, as you probably know, is just a surface emotion for pain."

How did a cowboy from Vermont understand everything that was going on in her head?

"Spent about three hundred hours workin' that nugget of wisdom out with my therapist," he said. "I think the therapy might have cost me more than the divorce attorney."

Ella laughed again, and this time, Jake joined her. To rid one's self of a spouse seemed a more expensive endeavor than actually acquiring one.

"Here we are." Just as he said the words, the horses quickened their gait around a bend in the road. Ella gasped at the sight before her; an open expanse of blanketed snow drifted in front of a three-story house. Rough-hewn, square-cut beams outlined the house, while river rock chimneys decorated both ends. White lights lined the snow-packed drive leading to the house, where more lights and giant wreaths and boughs of greenery decorated each of the dozen windows on the house.

"You live here?" Ella asked.

"You like it?" Jake asked.

"It's amazing," she said. *This* was why people loved winter. The whole scene could be lifted from a Norman Rockwell painting: the horses, the house, the cowboy ... the dog? A sudden thought pierced her consciousness.

"Am I dead?"

Jake turned to her, his eyebrows pulled together in an expression of puzzlement. "Not as far as I know," he said.

Ella pulled off a glove and bit down on her now-thawed

fingertip. A sharp pain went from finger to brain. She relaxed in the knowledge that she must be alive. But this night? The events seemed so random, and yet somehow so cohesive-- serendipitous.

Jake pulled to a stop in front of the massive front door to his spectacular home. He hopped out and helped Ella off the sleigh. Bovis stayed close to her side. Perhaps he, too, understood how perilously close they'd come to losing one another, and neither wished to suffer the loss. Two men in heavy coats and jeans strode outside. One picked up the reins to put up the horses, while the other listened as Jake instructed him as to the location of Ella's car.

Once they both left, Jake again turned his full attention to her. "Would you come in for a nightcap?"

Her now-tingly toes curled inside her boots. Was she ready for that? She sensed Jake's uniqueness in both lifestyle and demeanor. Her attraction, however, wasn't just to his money or his good looks; she was attracted in part to Jake because he mirrored that attraction back to her. She felt the frisson between them when he spoke, when they locked eyes, as he tucked her into the sleigh. The weight of his hand on her upper arm burned through her jacket and caused her to *want*.

"I ..." Ella was struck silent. How to answer?

He faced her. Both his hands held her steady. He sensed

her fears and her doubts. Her face gave away each of the emotions that raced through her mind.

"Ella," Jake said, the raspiness of his voice betraying his own desire. "I want you here for as long as you'd like to stay, but just so you know, I'm not going anywhere and it's an open invitation."

Her heart warmed with his simple and pure statement that she knew to be true.

"Woof!"

Ella jerked her gaze from Jake and toward Bovis. He now stood before Jake's front door his tail wagging fiercely.

"Woof!" Bovis barked again, and lifted his right front paw to scratch at the door to ensure his mistress realized his desires to enter.

"I think he wants in," Jake said.

"I guess so," Ella replied. She smiled knowing that, yes, she was ready for that nightcap and everything that might accompany the drink. She and Jake, his arm draped over her shoulder, walked toward Bovis. Her dog wiggled with excitement when Jake pulled open the door.

"You know," Ella said, "he's always been a really smart dog."

Snowflakes and Stones

By Malena Lott

He appeared in Moira's view as a colored spot among the crystal white landscape, his image growing larger as her Lexus crunched the snow on the red dirt road leading to the gate. She whispered his name, foreign on her tongue after such an absence: "Greyson." She'd forced herself to stop thinking of him every hour of the day the moment she'd signed the papers.

Her eyes shifted to her purse in the passenger seat, where she'd carefully tucked the papers amid the wadded-up Kleenex, abandoned lipstick tubes and pens without caps. He used to call her handbag the Bermuda Triangle. "Once it's in, it's not coming back out," he'd joked after countless scenes of her rummaging through it for lost sunglasses and car keys.

Planted next to a snowdrift, he wore faded denim jeans, a camel suede jacket and a black felt cowboy hat—the one he referred to as his "winter hat."

She blinked back tears at the sight of him, trying to push away the memories that flooded her mind. That hat had been

Layla's favorite. She'd climb on the rustic church pew in the entry hall and pluck it off the long hat rack. "Stick 'em up, pardner," Layla would say with her fingers crooked like a gun, the brim covering her brilliant blue eyes. Greyson and Moira would hold up their hands in mock fear until they all erupted in a fit of giggles on the living room floor.

It had been ten months since Moira had last seen him, ten months since she'd last been to Forever Ranch, the poorly named homestead of her husband's forefathers. *Ex,* she reminded herself. Soon, she'd have to start referring to him in the past tense.

What surprised her weren't the tears or the clench in her chest, but that she wanted Greyson to stay small in her heart, a speck of something that once was and could never be again. It was easier that way.

Her eyes had been so locked on Greyson that she hadn't noticed the much bigger presence behind the fence: Dasher and Dancer, the majestic Clydesdale horses, and the vintage English sleigh Greyson had spent two summers refurbishing after they got married. In times gone by, he would host sleigh rides for the townsfolk ten miles over. Moira had been in charge of hot chocolate, and Layla has passed out sugar cookies, wearing her green-and-white striped elf hat. Then it occurred to Moira that he could have taken up sleigh rides again. She couldn't assume to know anything about his life anymore.

Catching her breath, Moira contemplated turning the car around. Why had she agreed to meet him? Why hadn't she hired a courier to bring him the papers? And what kind of a woman would hand over divorce papers in lieu of a Christmas gift, even though he was expecting them?

Greyson's right hand lifted in a greeting, startling her. It wasn't uncommon. Everyday things made her jumpy, and she wasn't sure if anything could change that.

There was the smile that launched a thousand kisses and six years of matrimony. The smile that had told her they could grab life by the reins and ride into the sunset together. She blamed herself for believing him.

Before she knew it, he was at her door, opening it and helping her out, ever the gentlemen. No turning back now.

"Bags in the back?" he asked, and his voice reverberated in her ears like he spoke through a tunnel.

She realized she was staring at him, her mouth slack-jawed, his crystal-blue eyes still holding the same magnetic power they had since the first time she'd looked into them. "I hope she gets your eyes," Moira had whispered one morning toward the end of the pregnancy when they lay together on a lazy Sunday, Greyson rubbing his hand over her swollen belly.

Layla had inherited those baby blues, which made looking at him hurt all the more.

"Just one," she answered and popped open the trunk so he could retrieve it.

She listened for his retort—he'd never believe she could commit to a single bag for a long weekend—but when one didn't come, she reminded herself that he knew she had changed in ways big and small. Packing lighter was another sign that she'd mastered the art of shedding the past. She was a one-bag woman now, whether she liked it or not.

"I'm glad you're here," Greyson said as he hoisted her suitcase out of the trunk. The trunk door hid his face, but when he shut it and took a long look at her, she felt her throat squeeze.

"You look great. Better," he added.

She nodded, the only "thank you" she could muster. If possible, his rugged good looks had only intensified, but she wasn't about to compliment him. After all she'd put him through, she thought it best to say as little as possible.

"You hungry?" he asked, but didn't wait for an answer. "Jennifer made some of her chili. She's missed you."

Moira was thankful for the bitter cold wind to stop her tears in their tracks. When she'd left Greyson, she'd left her best friend, too. She had to cut all ties, even if it wasn't fair to Jennifer that she happened to be Greyson's younger sister.

They'd all learned life wasn't fair.

"Oh, I almost forgot," Moira said, reaching behind her seat to grab the lime-green and hot-pink polka-dotted package with the frilly, zebra-print bow.

"I don't even know what's inside, and I know she'll love it," Greyson said, closing the door behind her.

Dasher and Dancer raised their heads in greeting and clomped the snow. She liked to believe they'd missed her, too. She stroked their magnificent manes, a sense of calm coming over her. For a second, she imagined she might not only get through the weekend, but also enjoy it. Yet "joy" was the ornament at the top of tree, completely out of her reach. She'd simply stopped reaching.

She tried to get up into the sleigh herself, but like so much else, she faltered, and there he was, right behind her to hold her in his strong arms to lift her up. Her bum leg didn't help matters. After months of physical therapy, she could walk normally again, but tired easily.

"I've got it," she said, though she clearly didn't. She thought she heard a small sigh escape from his lips. How many times had she heard, "I'm only trying to help"?

Once in the front seat, Greyson covered her with the red-and-black-plaid blanket and whistled. "On Dasher, on Dancer," he said, which still made her smile. Layla had named them when she was two.

Moira soaked in the landscape, the rolling hills, hundred-year-old evergreens and the old barn that housed the menagerie of animals Layla had told everyone were her pets. "A ranch just isn't a ranch without a proper helping of beef, pork and chicken," Greyson had told Moira when he'd first suggested they leave their loft in the city for a quieter country life after his father left the homestead for Florida. "Just us and the sky," he'd told her.

"It's beautiful, isn't it?" he asked as the house and the billowing chimney smoke came into view. Snowflakes gently fell from above. Moira had forgotten gloves, but she didn't mind the cold. She held her finger out and caught a snowflake on its tip.

"How is each one different?" Layla had asked her when she was three.

"God's an artist," Moira had told her then, when she still believed. "No two are alike."

"What else?"

Moira had loved how Layla asked her the big questions without knowing they were big. "People and time. No two minutes are exactly the same, which is why you have to make every second count."

Then they'd thrown themselves on the ground and made snow angels until Greyson called them in.

"Moira?"

She realized they'd reached the circle drive, and the snowflake was gone. It struck her that all this time, she'd had it wrong, holding on to something that was impossible to bring back.

"It's breathtaking," Moira said, but beauty had never been the problem. Greyson was obviously still in love with this place, and no one could blame him. But for Moira, the open space, the very beauty she'd fallen in love with, had shown its ugly underbelly—the isolation and loneliness one can feel when you're in the middle of nowhere, and tragedy strikes.

The sky, with its changing palette of gorgeous hues, no longer worked to lift her mood. Neither had the changing leaves nor the whispering winds that did their best to pray her back to peace again. She needed the roar of the city, and so she left the sky, the trees and the menagerie, and finished breaking what was left of her shattered heart.

"Sleigh rides are on Sunday," Greyson told her as he pulled back the reins, slowing the sleigh to a stop. "You're special, so you got a sneak preview," he said, looking at her. He held her gaze, and she didn't feel the compulsion to look away.

Instinctively, she placed her hand over the scar on her cheek. He hadn't looked at it directly, but she knew he saw it all the same. After two surgeries, she felt less like

Frankenstein, but the scar would never fully go away, and she wasn't sure she wanted it to. It's not as though she needed a reminder—a punishment, perhaps? —but she didn't expect to look beautiful again when she felt so rotten inside.

"I'm glad I came," she said, and she meant it, then quickly added, "I think it's great you're doing the sleigh rides again. Family legacy and all."

Greyson's father and his father's father and *his* father's father had given them, too, making them the key backdrop in Christmas cards since the early 1900s. "It makes me happy to see them happy," Greyson said, and she knew by "they," he meant the families, and the children, in particular. Dasher and Dancer were bigger celebrities than any reindeer could hope for, and they joined four other Clydesdales on the ranch.

The rustic, double-front doors swung open and Greyson's family poured onto the porch with their usual good cheer. "Moira!" they yelled in chorus. She figured they were sizing her up, but her heart flooded with such love that she no longer cared about judgment.

Greyson's younger brother, Ben, the fireman; his wife, Tess; and their son, Charlie, took the lead. God, he would be four now, wouldn't he? "Auntie Moira!" Charlie yelled before jumping into her arms.

"Slow down, buddy," Ben said, leaning in to kiss Moira's cheek before peeling Charlie off her.

Yet she found her arms tightening around the child. *Four.* "It's fine. He's so big!" She hugged him and felt his tiny fingers around her neck, giving her goose bumps.

Inside, Greyson took her coat while Tess hooked her arm and led her to the fireplace. Greyson's father had spent four years planning the cabin before he'd built it thirty years earlier on the land his family had owned for a century. His meticulous attention and vision for a family gathering spot shined in every way, including the large stone fireplace where twenty guests could be seated around its immaculate hearth.

To her surprise, Greyson hadn't changed much in the house since she'd left, but the way things were had never gotten in the way of his ability to move on. The disintegration of their marriage, it seemed, was Moira's fault alone.

Greyson reappeared and handed her a cup of her old favorite: hot chocolate and espresso with a single miniature marshmallow. Moira thanked him, but found her throat closing up again as the tiny marshmallow melted on the surface of her drink. *How dare he?* she thought. Little things like lone marshmallows tracing back to an origin of happier times could send her off her rocker.

She took a sip, as good as she remembered, but the goodness of it all, the infusion of a family she'd left behind, and their outright happiness, overwhelmed her. *Breathe, Moira.*

Greyson stood at the edge of the room, as if contemplating where to sit. Was he purposefully giving her space, or, even worse, had moved on? Neither made her feel better. They deserved their holiday cheer, but for the time being, she had to get out of the room before it sucked her into the hearth like some sort of vortex. *Unhappy people don't belong here*, she told herself.

The package. It sat next to her on the faux-bearskin rug, its girliness out of place in such a masculine holiday setting. It was apparent Greyson had tried to decorate for the season without his sister's help. The "sparkles," as Layla had called them, were missing.

"I'll take this," Moira said, setting down her cup on the hearth and picking up the gift.

"She's in the kitchen," Greyson said, his smile faltering.

But she wasn't, though the half-eaten sugar cookies with extra red-and-green sprinkles were proof she'd been there. Moira blinked back tears and listened for the little girl's voice.

She followed the voice down the hall then stopped in her tracks. The bedroom. For some reason, she thought she could stay in the house and not ever have to step foot in it. She could call out, but they'd just holler for her to come in, wouldn't they?

Clearing her throat, she walked to the door, slightly ajar, and gently touched the hot-pink lettering on the door, spelling Layla's name above the corkboard her Aunt Jennifer had made her for her fourth birthday. The same photos were tucked in the pink ribbon: Layla with Dasher and Dancer; Layla and her "twin" cousin, Addy; and the last picture of them together as a family. Layla had her little arms wrapped around she and Greyson's necks, mashing their cheeks together. *That was it,* she thought, staring at the image of the woman who used to be Moira: that was the last time she'd truly been happy.

"Is someone there?" Jennifer called out from within the room.

Moira took a deep breath and pushed open the door and put on a weak smile. "I come bearing gifts," she said, holding out the package.

A tidal wave of emotion washed over her as she drank in the room. Like the rest of the house, it, too, was unchanged: the bumblebee garden painted on the left wall, the pink-and-yellow comforters with smiling bumblebees on the matching twin beds, and the art station in the corner that Greyson had built Layla when she was two.

Her white crib still anchored the other corner near the closet, but it wasn't empty.

Before she could take a peek, she was enveloped in hugs from Jennifer and Addy. "I knew you'd come!" Addy screamed. "I asked Santa for you to come back."

"I'm here," Moira said, her voice lifting in phony cheer. "And this is for the birthday girl!" She handed Addy the package, and the girl eagerly took it and set it on her bed, or the bed that used to be hers when they'd come to visit over the long summer break and every holiday, thereafter.

Jennifer didn't let go of Moira. "I asked Santa for you, too." She sniffled. "I didn't hear you drive up. I would've met you outside."

"Oh, I took the sleigh ride express," Moira said. "Besides, you have your hands full." She motioned to the crib, but still couldn't look inside. Jennifer looked well, plump and happy like every new-again mama should. Her amber hair was swept back into a ponytail, and her bright, blue eyes glistened with tears.

"Don't apologize," Jennifer said. "I'm too excited you're here to be mad at you right now."

They walked over to the crib, and inside laid the sweetest baby, fast asleep and making newborn noises.

Jennifer cleared her throat. "I wanted to send you a birth announcement, but Greyson said you'd moved again and hadn't left a forwarding address," Jennifer said. She reached for an envelope on the dresser and handed it to her.

Moira opened it and pulled out the thick card. *Layla Elisabeth. 8 lbs. 8 oz.*

"We call her Izzy," Jennifer said gently, as if to take the sting off, "but Addy insisted on naming her Layla. Did Greyson tell you?"

"He did," Moira said. Well, it *had* been on her voicemail, but that hadn't been his fault. She never picked up the phone for anyone. And like all the other times he'd called, she hadn't returned it, either.

"She's beautiful, Jen."

Moira reached down and stroked the baby's closed fist with her index finger.

"Can I open it now, Aunt Moira, pleeeease?" Addy begged from her spot on the bed.

"Sure, honey," Moira said, wiping a stray tear. She turned her attention to her niece, who was born only a month and two days after Layla. How could she be six already?

For all the ways Moira had tried to make time stand still, the world marched on. The minutes had all become dark clones, empty and sad, piling on top of each other until she could no longer lift the weight of her grief.

Addy had lost some of her baby fat, and she'd sprouted at least three inches since Moira had last seen her. They'd called the girls "twin" cousins because they shared many of the Thomas traits: the fine bone structure, wide smile, tipped nose with a sprinkling of freckles, and those big, blue eyes. Only Addy was a brunette like her mother, whereas Layla had been blonde.

Tearing open the package, Addy pulled out two stuffed animals—monkeys the girls had asked for the last time they'd all gone to the mall together, but, as usual, they were in a hurry, and the mothers promised they'd take the two back another time.

Addy squealed and hugged them tightly. "One for each bed," she said. "Do you think Layla would let Izzy play with hers?"

Moira bit her bottom lip and nodded. "Of course, sweetie."

Why had she done it? she wondered. Had two monkeys made instead of one? She'd only intended to get one for Addy when she'd stepped into the store two months earlier—on what would have been Layla's sixth birthday—but when the teenaged girl had asked which animal she'd wanted, she found herself blurting out "two" and pointing to the monkeys. She recalled Layla had said she wanted the pink outfit, and Addy wanted the purple one. There simply weren't many wishes she could make come true anymore.

"Thank you," Jennifer said, leaning her head on Moira's shoulder in a familiar move that best friends often do. "That must've been hard."

Moira nodded. Even brushing her teeth had been hard most days. Her therapist considered daily flossing a major step. "I got through it," Moira said, leaving out that she had cried at each station as the monkeys were put together, and she completely lost it when the plastic "hearts" were placed in the animals. The employees had sense enough not to ask her what the trouble was, but then, she figured she wore grief like a neon sign. Asking would be redundant.

Seeing Abby hug both of the monkeys, named "Olly" and "Tilly," made the trip worth it. *Milestone!* She could hear her therapist shrill in her ear. Moira began collecting them like rare coins.

"I didn't know what you needed for the baby," Moira said, handing Jennifer the gift card she'd tucked in her back pocket. The truth was that after the debacle at Build-a-Bear, she didn't dare walk into a baby store. They'd have to scoop her off the floor.

"Thank you," Jennifer said, hugging her friend and taking the card. "You hungry? I made your favorite. I even remembered the Tabasco."

"Famished," Moira said, following Abby and Jennifer out of the room while the baby slept.

Milestone! she shouted to herself in her mind. She'd made it through seeing the room again. How hard could a bowl of chili with her husband's family be?

His clan was already gathered around the ten-foot farm table. Greyson sat across from her. He would look at her the entire meal, turning her into mush. She would melt like the Wicked Witch, his warm stare the poison that would do her in.

No seats were left empty, thanks to cleverly pulling out the four leftovers. She couldn't bear empty chairs. "This is fine," she said, as she scooted in and put the holiday napkin on her lap. One glance at Greyson, and the memory hit her. "I can't go back to being a family of two," she'd said on her final night they'd eaten at the table. "We were supposed to be four, remember? And because of me, we're childless again."

She cleared her throat and took a long swig of wine. For a while, she'd turned to it to numb herself, but she'd found it easy to replace with food. So much so, that when she'd left Greyson, she'd been forty pounds heavier than the day of the accident. She'd tried starving herself at first – she barely ate for a month, and the hospital took to feeding her through a tube. Her life had become a pendulum wildly swinging from one end to the other. She'd been bone-thin; she'd been fat. It had become obvious she didn't care about her body long before she'd taken the midnight walk into the freezing pond.

"Greyson tells us you're swimming now," Ben said as he handed her the plate of cornbread.

She shook the memory. *Be here, now.* "Just at the Y," she answered. "About the only thing I can do quickly."

"Is that because you have a pin in your leg?" Charlie asked.

"Charlie!" Ben scolded.

"No, it's okay," Moira said. "Yes, Charlie, I do have a metal pin in my leg. I can't run anymore like I used to, so I swim like a fish." She puffed her cheeks out, causing Charlie to laugh.

"And you could be a pirate at Halloween with your scar," he said.

"Charles Benjamin Thomas!" his mother warned.

"It's fine, really. Do you remember the patch I had on my eye?" Moira asked.

Charlie nodded. "But your scar was bigger then."

"You were just two. That must've been scary for you to see. But it's better now, and who knows, maybe I *will* be a pirate someday." She hooked her hand and squinted her scarred eye, "Aargh, matey, gimme all your gold!"

The family laughed, reminding her of the days when she had been the life of the party—"the entertainer," Greyson had called her.

"You're funny, Aunt Moira. I should take you to show-and-tell, but my class always wants to see my dad in his firefighter uniform." Charlie rolled his eyes.

Ben ruffled his son's hair. "Hey, you not proud of your old man?"

"Yeah, but the scar is cooler."

Greyson cleared his throat. "Okay, that's enough, Charlie."

The baby started crying in the bedroom. Jennifer scooted her chair back, but Moira put her hand on her arm to stop her. "May I?"

"Are you sure? I mean, absolutely! Her bottle's in the warmer in her room." Jennifer said.

Izzy's wail grew louder upon seeing Moira, but as soon as she was in her arms, the baby began rooting.

"Nothing in there," Moira said, grabbing the bottle with her free hand. Holding Izzy, she felt something stir inside, like rusty, old gears cranking again.

To her surprise, it was still there: the maternal instinct that told her how to hold the baby, to sing softly, to rock in the chair. For some reason, she thought she'd never do any of those things again. Her Three Kings of Misery—anger, guilt and resentment—had not followed the star to Layla's room.

While rocking, she sang some of Layla's favorite lullabies. She hadn't noticed she had an audience.

"She likes you," Greyson said in the doorway.

"She'd like anyone with a bottle," Moira answered with a shrug, and thankfully the four-ounce bottle was almost empty. She removed the nipple from Izzy's mouth and put the baby over her shoulder to burp.

"Remember how Layla refused to burp?" Moira asked. "I swore she was doing it just so I'd hand her off to you, the burping champ."

"Well, she just liked hearing me burp with her," he said. "But it was Uncle Ben who taught her how to burp her ABCs."

Moira laughed. "It worked, though. She got a gold star in pre-K that day. Thankfully reciting it without the burps."

"I loved hearing you sing," he said. "And saying her name."

Moira smiled, but she couldn't look at Greyson for long. She stayed silent; the only sound in the room her hand patting the baby's back and their breathing. That's what had gotten the best of her before: the aching, omniscient silence.

She closed her eyes and could hear the dining room erupt in laughter time and again—the happy ones. True, there'd been a couple of months when she'd asked Greyson not to talk about Layla or the unborn child they'd lost. The very things she had loved about Greyson early on—his charisma, his optimistic outlook and talkative nature—felt like weapons after the accident. Not that he didn't grieve—Lord, did he grieve! —but hearing the father of her children cry over them only made her feel guiltier. After the third night of listening to his moans from the other room—hours on end! —she'd decided to take that moonlight stroll over the ice.

"I'm signing over the house to Jennifer and Mark," he said, as if confessing.

"Oh?" *Surprise.* "But you love it here. Where will you go? Never mind. I don't deserve to ask that."

"Deserve? I'm thrilled you want to know."

"I can't say I'm not curious."

"Curious is ... curious is nice," he said, looking at her sideways. Did he find it difficult to look at her, too?

"I'm just ... is it another woman? A new job? Maybe it'll be good for you to get away.

Greyson put his head on his hands and ran his fingers through his hair – his usual sign of frustration with his wife. *Well, he wouldn't have to be frustrated with her much longer,* she thought.

"I'm not *running away*," he said, finally.

"What ... like I did? With my leg, it was more like I zombie-shuffled away."

He shook his head. "I can't be upset with you when you make jokes like that. And that pirate impression. That was something else." He laughed. "It feels good to have you back. I mean, to have you here."

She knew what he'd meant. "Greyson, there's something I need to tell you. Something I had to say in person. I've lived in a fog for so long that I couldn't see what I was doing to you. This may not make sense, and it was wrong of me to just leave like I did, but I couldn't stand putting you through putting up with me any longer. And, as for not returning your calls, I just couldn't. I had to learn how to take care of myself."

He nodded slowly. "I'd been expecting a Dear John letter long before I found it, but I still preferred it over the alternative." His voice cracked.

She knew what he'd meant by that, too. "Thank you for inviting me. I wanted to apologize in person."

"Working through steps?"

"Steps? Oh, well, nothing formal, anyway. Ann calls them 'milestones.' Some are big stones and some are small stones. And, some, like coming here, are friggin' *boulders*."

"Whatever brought you here, I'll take it." His expression softened, and she saw in him what had always been, what she'd given up, time and again. How many minutes had she lost with the living?

Moira pressed her cheek against the baby's warm back. "I suppose the only measuring stick I have for my progress is to be around the people who used to mean the most to me. I've been avoiding Jennifer because I couldn't bear to see Addy grow up and know what Layla would've looked like now. But when I saw Addy today, it wasn't so bad. I have to start seeing the world as it is, instead of how the world would've been."

She cleared her throat. Her heart beat crazily. She used to not care how her words stung him, but she could hear her speech echoing through the room.

Greyson clasped his hands and looked at the floor. "There isn't another woman," he said. "It's a job at the university. I finished my master's so ..."

"A professor! You did it!" Her enthusiasm surprised even herself. Where had that come from?

He puffed his chest. "Just an associate professor now, but we'll see how it goes."

Moira smiled, genuinely happy for him. "Isn't that something?" She paused, readjusting the puzzle pieces in her head, setting Greyson and his future life far away from hers.

"There's one more thing," she said. "I met her. In person. Last month."

Greyson's eyes widened, and then moistened. "I'm glad. Do you see that she's not a monster?"

Moira placed her hand on his arm. "She's a good girl. Graduates from college in May. She's traveled the whole tri-state area on campuses talking about what happened. I see how it hurt her. She cried. I cried. But, unlike me, she didn't let it destroy her. I don't see how anyone who hears her story would text and drive again."

"And you? Tell me you don't still blame yourself," he said, putting his hand over hers.

"It's a mother's job to see what's coming," she said, peeling her hand away. "I better turn in." She kissed Izzy on the forehead. "I'll let the burp champ finish the job."

"Goodnight, M."

"Goodnight, Grey."

She let the tenor of his voice hum in her ear as she made the short walk down the hall to the guest room. It was the first time they'd said "goodnight," but wouldn't be sleeping in the same bed.

As she slipped under the blankets, she gave herself two internal cheers: *milestone, milestone!* One for holding a baby and not breaking down, and the other for talking reasonably with her husband and not a) fighting, or b) jumping his bones. In the past, she'd been very good at both.

It wasn't just the family that lured Moira back to the cabin at Christmastime, but a yearning for all of her senses to come back to life. Like smells: the hickory in the fireplace, the crisp pine of the eight-foot Christmas tree, the amber musk of the bedding, and the pop of frying bacon. Lots and lots of bacon.

She awoke early to find she'd had the best sleep she'd had in months. Thanks to keeping the window cracked open—an old habit—she'd buried herself beneath the comforters while fresh air swirled in the room, a siren song that caused her to sleep soundly all night without a single nightmare. No screeching wheels or broken glass or sirens coming for her in the distance.

Almost despite herself, she slipped into her old rituals: three packages of bacon, two dozen eggs, cinnamon toast with extra butter —ah, the smell of cinnamon, how had she forgotten it? —and the sharp, citrus scent of fresh-squeezed orange juice. Only when she was done with her breakfast feast did she realize it was 5:30 a.m. and the family wouldn't be up for an hour or more.

She contemplated getting Jennifer up so they could have coffee—Lord, those aromatic beans, freshly ground!— but Jennifer had likely been up and down all night with the baby and needed her sleep. Her next thought was to wake Greyson—strange how she had to fight the urge to do it.

What would she say to him, and he to her? Maybe he'd ask her about her dreams like he used to before they all turned into nightmares.

Instead, she wrapped up in her coat and decided she'd watch the sunrise out back and then come in and reheat the food when the family awoke.

It had snowed during the night, leaving a fresh coat of powder over the deck and Adirondack chairs. She stood at the railing, breathing in the new day and filling her lungs with the frigid air. A doe stood in the field, still as a statue, staring at her. It blinked. She blinked.

The doe turned its head toward the batch of evergreens and darted for cover. Squirrels raced through the trees. Birds twittered and shared berries. In the distance, she heard Dasher and Dancer and the other Clydesdales in their luxury stables. She decided she'd take care of the morning chores so Greyson wouldn't have to.

Her boots crunched through the snow, but she'd greatly underestimated the extra inches that accumulated overnight, which made it seem much farther and the trek nearly impossible. Her bad leg began to ache, beginning at her hip and sending shooting pain down to her feet. Even with her swimmer's lungs, she was out of breath.

She'd only made it to the pond, barely halfway to the stables, yet the sun glowed in the horizon, making her walk a brighter journey. She closed her eyes and felt the warmth of the new sun on her face—kissing her eyelids, her nose, her cheeks, her mouth. When she opened them again, she realized she was at the water's edge. A family of ducks swam before her—a mother and her two ducklings.

It's just nature, she told herself, trying not to read anything into it. She'd taken such normalcy and exaggerated it for self-pity in the past, but she had to let go of that, too. Mothers would go on mothering, and mothers without their young had to go on, too.

She'd been so transfixed on the ducks that she hadn't heard the heavy breathing or the clomp of feet in the snow behind her. When Greyson reached her, she nearly fainted from surprise.

"Moira! What are you doing out here!" he stood before her, his face red from the bitter wind, and his jacket open, revealing he had thrown it on in haste over his plaid pajamas. One pajama leg was tucked in a boot, the other bunched up at his knee.

Only then did she feel the cold on her face, how chapped her hands had become. She hadn't thought to put on gloves or a hat. When she opened her mouth, her face felt tight, like a mask. "Oh," she said, before her teeth began to chatter. The panicked expression on Greyson's face told the story he'd conjured, and how the clues of her carelessness as she stood transfixed in front of the pond must've resulted in his mad dash.

"Oh, God, Moira," he said, panting and then bent over, clutching his knees and gasping for breath as a guttural sob filled the air.

"No, it's not what you think!" she said, putting her hand on his shoulder and then her other hand on his head, pulling him to her chest. He wrapped his arms around her waist.

"I just came out for a minute," she explained, "but then there was a doe and then the ducklings in the water." But she looked over and the ducks were no longer in the pond. Had Greyson scared them away, or were they never there in the first place?

He stood and cradled her face in his hands. "The smell of bacon woke me up. When I went to the kitchen and saw it, and then saw you standing at the pond, I assumed—"

"That I'd made a final offering?" She smiled. "You know how I hate wasting good food. You'd never eat it if I offed myself!"

"Dammit, Moira. I don't know what to think, anymore. You seemed so calm last night. So at peace. And you apologized. They say that people are happiest right before ..."

Moira took Greyson's large, warm hand and kissed his palm. "I just woke up in a semi-good mood for once. You damn happy people are rubbing off on me."

"Can we please get the hell back in the cabin and warm up?"

She let go of him, but found she didn't want to. He kissed her forehead and hugged her tighter as they walked up the slope back to the cabin. Inside, the kitchen was still empty with the cooling feast awaiting slumbering guests. The clock struck 6 a.m.

"If you can't beat 'em, join 'em," Greyson said with a yawn, as he peeled off his coat and headed back to his bedroom. He paused and turned back to face her. "I couldn't sleep last night," he said. "It felt wrong."

She knew what that meant, too: in the same house, but not in the same bed.

Without thinking, without overanalyzing or questioning, she followed her heart, which led her directly to him. She stood at his doorway and watched him settle into bed, his broad back to her as he nestled under the burgundy comforter. She felt the tug of a smile and walked to his bed —their bed—and climbed under the covers. She put her hand through the space between his waist and his arm. He held her hand and squeezed it, his warmth transferring to her.

No two minutes are alike, she thought.

Her cheek against his shoulder, she asked softly, "Still?" and he didn't hesitate before turning to embrace her.

"Forever."

About the Authors

Megan Barlog, 22, will graduate from California State University, Northridge, in December 2011 with a degree in English and an emphasis in Creative Writing. Her short story "The Escape" is her first publication, and if she has anything to say about it, it won't be her last. She lives in California with her parents, two sisters, two brothers, and a skittish dog named Casey.

Maria Geraci is the author of *The Boyfriend of the Month Club*, *Bunco Babes Gone Wild* and *Bunco Babes Tell All*. The married, mother-of-three lives in Florida, and is currently working on her next novel. www.mariageraci.com

Maggie Marr is the author of *Hollywood Girls Club* and *Secrets of the Hollywood Girls Club*. The writer/producer lives in Los Angeles with her husband, and is currently working on a contemporary romance and a new motion picture script. www.maggiemarr.com

Malena Lott is the author of several novels including *Fixer Upper* and *Dating da Vinci*, and the ebook novella, *Life's a Beach*. The married Oklahoman mama-of-three is a brand strategist and founder of Buzz Books and the group blog BookEndBabes.com. www.malenalott.com

Jenny Peterson was the lifestyles editor for the Oklahoma Gazette before she and her husband became new Coloradans in the fall of 2011. She writes young adult fiction in her spare time. www.jennycoonpeterson.com

Dani Stone is a freelance writer juggling assignments like a circus performer in sparkly red shoes. Currently, she's contributing web content for MediaRefined.com and writing a charity spotlight series for the life-changing micro-giving site, Lovedrop.us. Dani lives with her husband and two children in the great flat state of Kansas. www.ihearlaughtracks.wordpress.com

Samantha Wilde is the author of *This Little Mommy Stayed Home* and a graduate of Concord Academy, Smith College and Yale Divinity School. A yoga teacher and minister by training, and a stay-at-home mother by calling, she writes during nap times at her home in Massachusetts where she lives with her husband and three children. www.samanthawilde.com

Author Recipes

Grammy's Monkey Bread by Megan Barlog
Ingredients:
2 cans refrigerated buttermilk biscuits
¼ cup butter, melted
¾ cup sugar 1 tablespoon cinnamon
¼ cup chopped pecans

Directions:
1. Heat oven to 375 degrees.
2. Grease an 8" round cake pan.
3. Separate biscuits and dip in butter.
4. Coat entire biscuit with mixture of sugar and cinnamon.
5. Place coated biscuit in pan. Repeat until you have placed 15 to 16 biscuits in pan. Biscuits should be around outer edge of pan and overlap to fill in center.
6. Pour rest of butter over top.
7. Sprinkle with nuts.
8. Bake 25 to 30 minutes.

Nutmeg Squash by Jenny Peterson
Ingredients:
Cubed butternut squash (about 4 cups)
4 tbsp. butter
1 tbsp. brown sugar
1/2 tsp. ground nutmeg
1/2 tsp. salt

Directions:
Bring the squash to a boil until tender (about 15 minutes). Drain and beat the squash and add in everything else. Easy peasy!

Cranberry Pecan Jell-O Salad by Dani Stone
Ingredients:
1 stick butter or margarine
1 cup flour
1 cup chopped pecans
1 - 8 Oz. package cream cheese
1 cup sugar
1 – 12 oz. Cool Whip
1 – 6 oz. box of cranberry Jell-O
2 cups boiling hot waster
2 16 oz. cans whole cranberry sauce

Directions:
1. In a 9" by 13" pan, melt 1 stick of butter or margarine. Mix in 1 cup of flour and 1 cup of chopped pecans. Press evenly in pan and bake at 350º for 12-15 minutes. Cool.
2. Mix cream cheese and 1 cup sugar. Fold in Cool Whip. Spread on cooled crust.
3. Dissolve Jell-O in water and mix in cranberries. Refrigerate until thickened. Pour over cream cheese layer.
4. Refrigerate until firm and ready to serve.

My mother-in-law makes this every Thanksgiving. We serve it on a piece of endive lettuce on its own little plate. The salad is a gorgeous, tasty addition to any table.

Christmas Breakfast Casserole by Malena Lott
Ingredients:
1 package hot and spicy or mild sausage
6 eggs
6 slices of buttered bread
2 cups of milk
1 package of shredded cheddar cheese

Directions:
1. Brown and crumble sausage; drain and set aside.
2. In a large bowl, beat eggs; add milk.
3. Spray casserole dish with a non-stick spray. Lay six pieces of buttered bread on the bottom.
4. Pour mixture over the bread.
5. Add the crumbled sausage then top with the cheese.
6. Cover and place in the fridge overnight.
7. Next morning, remove from the fridge and pre-heat oven to 350.
8. Bake, uncovered, at 350 degrees F for 40 minutes or until a knife inserted near the center comes out clean.

Filling and delish!

Acknowledgments

If I could, I would have a custom sleigh ride made big enough to fit all of these VIPs in it. Hot cocoa with mini-marshmallows for each of you!

- My friends, family and readers
- My husband who is also a phenom editor!
- My Book End Babes and Girlfriend Book Club authors
- My Twitter followers and Facebook friends and Instagram pals
- My fellow authors in this book. It would not be a "collection" without you!
- Alpha Chi Omega for inspiring me and developing young women leaders
- My kids, Harrison, Audrey and Owen, for knowing I would be cranky if I didn't write

Winter blessings!